PARTY FAVORS

A So Over the Holidays Novella

ERIN MCLELLAN

Content Warnings: explicit sex and language; alcohol consumption; slightly controlling parents

Bottle Rocket (So Over the Holidays #3)

"Scorching hot! Bottle Rocket *is a story of sexual awakening that fed my femdom fantasies."*

   —New York Times bestselling author Skye Warren

"Erin McLellan does it again with a sexy, Independence Day-themed romp ... You'll be cheering for Rosie, Leo, and their summer of love as they get a second chance at happily ever after, fireworks included."

   —Layla Reyne, author of the bestselling Fog City Trilogy

"This sexy, fun, LGBTQ sex-positive series continues with another great installment! I loved the banter between the hero and heroine, loved the fast pace, and McLellan's trademark humor and great characterization. This is a solid homerun for me!"

   —Annabeth Albert, author of the Hotshots Series

Candy Hearts (So Over the Holidays #2)

"Candy Hearts *by Erin McLellan is sweet, steamy, totally cute and little bit kinky.*"

—National Public Radio (For February, 3 Romances That Are Short and Candy-Sweet)

"*A super swoon Valentine's Day read with the perfect mix of spice, sweetness, and humor.*"

—Neve Wilder, author of the Rhythm of Love Series

"Candy Hearts *is blazing hot Valentine's fun that is jam packed with delightful tropes and sex toys. Exactly the level of heat I needed to melt the winter blues.*"

—Rachel Reid, author of the Game Changers Series

Stocking Stuffers (So Over the Holidays #1)

"*Erin McLellan delivers an authentic portrait of a bisexual woman embarking on a M/F relationship …* Stocking Stuffers *belongs in the stocking of any romance reader looking for a fresh take on holiday romance with a healthy side of kink.*"

—Entertainment Weekly (19 Christmas Romances to Keep You Warm This Holiday Season)

Blurb

Three…

Amanda Ellis knows three things: she's tired of doing what's expected of her, she hates her job at her family's business, and the last thing she wants to do is attend her parents' boring New Year's Eve ball with a date her mother picked. A few days of fun with her online best friend is exactly what she needs to ring in the New Year on her own terms.

Two…

Wren Rebello is impulsive and always ready for fun. A last-minute girls' getaway sounds like the perfect way to spend New Year's. But even Wren isn't prepared for the spark of attraction she feels when she meets Amanda in person for the first time. Good thing Wren loves popping Amanda's cork.

One…

After days spent sharing end-of-year resolutions and the one bed in their cottage, the clock strikes midnight and the ball drops on their time together. As Amanda and Wren go their separate ways, they leave new resolutions unfulfilled. Is there enough New Year's magic left to turn their online friendship into real-life love?

To everyone who needs a little hope this New Year's.

Prologue

March

Wren: *Guess who has 2 thumbs and another breakup on the books.*

    Amanda: *Oh no! What happened?*

Wren: *Same old, same old.*

Wren: *I'm too wild.*

Wren: *I'm messy and impulsive and indulgent.*

    Wren: *I don't take things seriously, so therefore … it wasn't serious.*

    Wren: *The usual.*

    Amanda: *That's bullshit. You're fun. If people can't handle being with someone fun, then they suck. It's not on you.*

    Wren: *You're just saying that because you're my friend. You have to.*

    Amanda: *I'm saying it because you're a bright spot in my life, and we've never even met. It pisses me off when people who get you in person take you for granted.*

    Wren: *Gah, you're too nice.*

Wren: *I'm going to sew myself a ridiculous leather corset to make myself feel better. Wanna see?*

Amanda: *Yes.*

July

Amanda: *Hey, it's our friendship anniversary. You DM'd me exactly five years ago for the first time.*

Wren: *FRIENDSHIPVERSARY!*

Wren: *Just think, it's only been 1825 days since you sold me a 1950s teddy pattern on Twitter. Feels like yesterday.*

Wren: *We should celebrate. Fly out here. We'll have a party. Or I'll fly out there.*

Amanda: *LOL*

Wren: *We'll get drunk.*

Wren: *I'll buy us those little noise thingies you blow into.*

Wren: *Or sashes with our names on them. Or tiaras that say, "Best Gal Pals."*

Amanda: *I do love a good tiara. Maybe next year. Did I tell you I've been summoned to another charity auction? Can't remember the cause. Something to do with pigeons? Anyway, my mom bought me a dress. It's a very respectable greige. She didn't want me to wear one of my "vintage pieces of trash."*

Wren: *Ohhh. Hot.*

Wren: *I bet your vintage piece of trash would be 10x better than anything that's fucking greige.*

Amanda: *Thanks.*

Wren: *Did she summon a date for you as well?*

Amanda: *I'll have you know that I'm quite interested in Dr. Ned Applebaum III. We have a lot in common.*

Wren: *Bullshit.*

Amanda: *Yep. You win some, you lose some. I seem to lose most.*

September

Wren: *I missed you while you were on vacation.*

Wren: *That's a dumb thing to say, huh?*

Wren: *It's not like we see each other every day or anything, but we usually talk every day. And I missed you.*

Wren: *Blah. Ignore me. I'm hungover.*

Amanda: **Passes the virtual Tylenol and greasy eggs**

Amanda: *I missed you too.*

December

Wren: *Ready for recent Tinder pickup lines?*

Wren: *This one is from Kyle, 28. He wrote, "If your left leg is Thanksgiving and your right leg is Christmas, can I visit between the holidays?"*

Amanda: *OMG. Did you block him?*

Wren: *No. I told him, "Only if you do it mouth first."*

Wren: *He agreed, but this time of year is busy, so he hasn't gotten a chance to prove himself.*

Amanda: *My mother gave a man my number because she is super helpful. (Eyeroll) He sent me this text yesterday: "Wanna meet Santa's little helper?" accompanied by a dick pic.*

Wren: *Oof.*

Wren: *What's with the dick pics?*

Wren: *I want ballsack pics or nothing at all.*

Amanda: *LOL. I should swear off dating people my mother picks out for me next year. Maybe I'd actually get an orgasm at the hands of someone besides myself.*

Wren: *Ooo Ooo Ooo. New Year's Eve resolutions for Amanda Ellis. I like this game.*

Amanda: *Wait, that's not what I said.*

Wren: *Speed dating.*

Amanda: *…*

Wren: *More sex toys.*

Wren: *Hire one of those matchmakers for rich people.*

Amanda: *Wren! OMG.*

Wren: *I'm proud of that last one.*

Wren: *More sex toys.*

Amanda: *You already said that.*

Wren: *It's the best one.*

Amanda: *Not sure I believe in NYE resolutions. New Year's is a pointless holiday. Like Groundhog Day. No purpose. I always try to set goals and resolutions, but they put me on a fast track to failure instead. Also, I've NEVER had a fun New Year's Eve. Ever. The whole concept is a scam.*

Wren: *Oh, pretty girl, I'm going to prove you wrong.*

Chapter One

You should never meet your heroes. Amanda believed that with her whole heart. Once, when she was twelve, she'd met a boy bander whose poster she had on her wall. It was one of those early formative moments. He'd treated her, and the other screaming preteens, like they were frivolous and silly and nothing special.

Well, today Amanda had flown six hours to meet her online best friend in person for the first time, and she was worried this plan would go the way of that adage about heroes. Except Amanda wasn't concerned that Wren Rebello would be horrible or any different than she was online, which was funny, fierce, and kind. No, Amanda was scared shitless that *she*—Amanda Ellis, the disco ball heiress—would be pegged as nothing special. *Again.*

The Father Time Farm and Resort loomed large in front of her, but she was nervous to go inside. According to the resort's website, the grounds were littered with cottages, gardens, and orchards, all of which were covered in a dusting of snow that had blown in just in time for the end-of-year celebrations. The big lodge that she could see through her rental car windshield housed an indoor pool, sauna, and spa, two highly rated restaurants, a bar, an event hall, and several floors of rooms.

Wren Rebello was waiting for her at the indoor pool with a few of Wren's super cool, super successful, super supportive friends.

This whole New Year's Eve girls' getaway had been Wren's idea. A spur-of-the-moment idea, which, after five years of online friendship, Amanda knew was how most of Wren's ideas came about.

They had talked about meeting for years, but Amanda had thought it was just that—*talk*. A fairy tale. A story they had dreamed up but never intended to actually write down.

Amanda was that type of predictable. She did what was expected of her in the family business because she was the perfect daughter. She dated the right type of guy, went to the correct events, wore the clothes her mom picked out. She followed her daily routine to a tee: coffee, treadmill, yoga, work, lunch, work, snack, message with Wren, dinner, TV time, bed. She dreamed of making changes, chasing dreams, doing something wild and rash and *different* for once in her life, but she'd never followed through.

Wren followed through.

Wren had emailed her a week ago: *Do you know what I need? To finally have that girls' getaway with my online bestie. That's you, by the way, in case that wasn't clear. I've got a two-*

bedroom cottage at Father Time Farm and Resort booked from Dec. 29 to Jan. 1 and a New Year's Eve party ticket with your name on it. A few of my other friends will be there, but they're all disgustingly coupled up. Please please please? I'm alone for New Year's. You're alone for New Year's. Let's be alone together.

The problem was that Amanda wasn't supposed to be alone for New Year's Eve. She was supposed to escort the honorable Mr. Thatcher Aldridge to her parents' annual Midnight Charity Ball. Her mother had set it up, of course. The Aldridges were old tech money, whatever that meant, and Thatcher was the marrying age. Didn't matter that Thatcher was a dick-pic-sending sleazeball who thought Amanda was nothing more than a mannequin for his arm.

Amanda couldn't handle the bullshit for another night. She needed a break. She needed a real New Year's Eve. A New Year's Eve like the ones in movies with the countdown and the champagne and the glitter and the *friends*.

Her mother sending her a picture of the taupe evening gown she'd selected for Amanda had been the final freaking straw.

So, she'd lost her entire damn mind, sent a text to her parents, a *fuck you* to Thatcher Aldridge, and jumped on a plane.

She was here now, about to meet her online best friend. A woman she messaged with every day but whose voice she'd never heard. A woman who made her every day brighter and better but didn't truly know Amanda at all. It was so easy to hide the scared or boring parts when you could curate your every word, every thought.

No turning back. She had to face the music.

She dragged her bags to the front desk. The lodge was leaning a bit too hard into the Scandinavian après-ski aesthetic if you asked her, especially as there were no ski hills in sight, but it was nice, cozy, and clean. There was a ton of light filtering in through huge windows and a skylight in the atrium near the entrance.

She'd gotten a text from Wren an hour ago with an update: *So excited for you to get here. This place is a gem. Our cottage is great, but it came with a funny surprise in the second bedroom. Your key is with the concierge. William, Benji, and I are going to head to the pool. If you get here soon, find us there!*

Amanda knew all about Benji, the Instagram lingerie model, and William, a nightclub owner and Wren's IRL best friend. Wren talked about them constantly and said they were soulmates. Amanda was jealous, and she'd never laid eyes on the guys.

"My friends told me they're at the pool. Could you point me in that direction?" Amanda asked the worker at the front desk after he checked her in.

"Through that hallway, go down a flight of stairs at the end, and then follow the wooden arrow signs. You'll see it. There's not much down there."

Amanda drummed her fingers on the desk. "Could I leave my bags here for a few minutes? I'll swing back by for them after I say hi."

"Of course. We could deliver them to your cottage if you would prefer."

"That won't be necessary. Thank you."

Amanda's heart was in her throat when she found a wooden sign pointing toward the pool, sauna, and spa. Everything was muggy, steam billowing around her feet as she stepped into the room with the pool. The scent of chlorine assaulted her. The pool itself wasn't overly busy, but there were lots of people milling about. On the far side of the room was a glass wall with views of the forest covered in snow.

Amanda immediately second-guessed herself about *everything* as she took a step closer to the water—coming here, meeting Wren, changing the dynamic of their friendship, wearing this getup (her favorite high-heeled boots, skirt, and white wool swing coat) down to the pool.

Wren was so fun. A badass lingerie designer, confident, open, and funny. And Amanda was the heir to a company that had made a small fortune manufacturing disco balls in the '70s. She closely guarded her feelings and thoughts. Hell, Wren didn't even really know what Amanda looked like. She'd been using the same profile picture for five years. Her hair was a totally different color, and she wasn't twenty-three anymore.

"Amanda? Is that you?" a voice with a slight drawl called from the opposite side of the pool.

Amanda searched out the owner of that voice, and when she found it, the heat in the room made her dizzy. At least, she was blaming the heat. Wren was across the pool sitting with her feet in the water.

Amanda sometimes studied pictures of Wren on Instagram. She had an interesting, expressive face that probably drew *everyone* in, made *everyone* click on her pictures, even if they didn't have an account. Amanda had seen photos of Wren in her usual punky, rock-star attire—combat boots, tight jeans, loose T-shirts, leather jackets.

Now, Wren was all skin, and slicked-back wet hair, and a tiny black two-piece, and glistening water droplets, and a smile so big Amanda wanted to drown in it. She felt like a flurry of champagne bubbles had burst in her veins at once.

Holy shit.

Amanda took a wobbly step toward Wren, but she wasn't watching where she planted her foot, too preoccupied by the pull of *looking* versus *not looking*.

Her toe and heel should have planted on the weird, textured cement surrounding the pool. Instead, she hit air. Then water. She tried to catch herself, flinging her purse in the process, but it didn't work.

She tumbled into the pool. The *deep end* of the pool.

She went under and thought about staying down there. It would be nice to take a moment to live in the reality that existed before she resurfaced. Before she was the woman who fell into a pool the first time she met Wren Rebello in person because she'd been surprised by an inconvenient zip of attraction.

Happy New Year to her bisexuality.

It was time to wrap those feelings up and ignore them like a regifted white elephant present.

It wasn't the first time Amanda had seen a woman

and thought, "Wow. *Yes*. That." But it didn't happen that often, so when it did, she felt it keenly.

Strong arms reached her and started to tug her toward the surface. She helped them by kicking her legs. It wasn't like she was drowning, just drowning in embarrassment. She surfaced and came face to face with Wren for the first time. All that skin she'd been perving on before tumbling into the pool in front of dozens of people was against her.

"Oh my hot damn, Amanda. Are you all right? I've got you. I'll help you."

Amanda let Wren help her because it was nice. She didn't tell Wren that she had been an All-State swimmer in high school because that would have required full sentences, and Amanda was too mortified to attempt that.

Wren kept her hand on Amanda's back as Amanda climbed the ladder at the edge of the pool. Her coat was heavy and stuck to her legs, and her boots were full of water. A man helped her take the last step out of the pool.

"Hi, I'm Benji. That was hilarious. Are you okay?"

The man standing slightly behind Benji, William presumably, covered his eyes with his palm.

"I'm fine," she said. "Just, you know, humiliated. I'm Amanda."

"We've heard a lot about you. Glad you could save Wren from a few days of being a third wheel."

"Oh shush, Benji," Wren said.

Amanda took her coat off. It was sopping. Her cream-colored top was also soaked … and see-through.

Wren corralled Amanda toward a lounge chair and

magicked a fluffy white robe out of nowhere, wrapping it around Amanda without asking.

Amanda stared at Wren, and Wren stared back. Wren was shorter than her by a good half a foot, but her charisma seemed to fill the room. Or indoor pool. A slow, devastatingly ornery smile pulled at Wren's lips.

Coming here for New Year's had been the right decision, if only to see that smile.

Chapter Two

Amanda Ellis was blonde. Wren's brain kept snagging on that point. In her profile picture on Twitter, her hair was a creamy, caramelly brown, and that was the only picture Wren had ever seen. But now, Amanda's hair was blonde and very long. Wren liked it that way, all golden and sunshiny.

Amanda was also tall and curvy. Her legs looked a mile long in those fancy black boots with the spiked heels, and her skin was sun-kissed.

Basically, she was intimidatingly pretty even with melting mascara making a mess of her face.

Wren wasn't easily intimidated, though, and nothing in the world would keep her from running full speed ahead into this time with Amanda Ellis. Wren had wanted this for so long. Had wanted to see if the butterflies she'd felt for years when her phone lit up with messages from Amanda transferred to seeing Amanda's smile. To being in the same time zone as her.

It was odd, though. There was a disconnect in Wren's brain. She knew Amanda so well. She knew Amanda's hopes and dreams. She knew Amanda fantasized about ditching the family business for good. She knew Amanda hated to be called the disco ball heiress. They shared their daily triumphs and disappointments. Amanda treated Wren like she was more than the wild child or the party girl. Amanda made Wren feel special with nothing but a DM. But Wren had never heard Amanda's voice. Wren didn't know Amanda's hair color. It was a bit of a mindfuck.

But Wren didn't need to know the physical things about Amanda to know she had an annoyingly huge crush on her.

The physical things were pretty nice, though.

"Let's get you back to our cottage to rinse off, warm up, and change," Wren suggested. Amanda nodded and stood up. Her clothes were still dripping.

"We're going to keep swimming," William said. "Should we meet at the bar before dinner? Say six thirty?"

"Sure. See you then," Wren said.

They swung by the front desk to grab Amanda's bags, getting a few funny glances. Wren was giving the lobby a show in her swimsuit. She'd forgotten to grab a towel or a robe when they'd left the pool, which sucked, considering they had to walk down a snowy garden path to get to their cottage.

"I'm glad you're here," Wren said as they exited the lodge. Wren had wanted this so badly. She'd thought about it for ages before pulling the trigger and begging Amanda to come. She was normally impulsive, but this had been cooking in her brain for years.

"I feel like a walking, talking disaster so far." Amanda was staring straight ahead, not meeting Wren's eyes. Her teeth were chattering.

"Nah. It's been great. Nothing breaks the ice like fallin' in a pool."

A chuffing little chuckle escaped Amanda's mouth. She was wearing pink lipstick that hadn't been ruined by her wet tumble, and her lips seemed plump and juicy. And ... Wren needed to stop staring before she made it weird.

It was just that every once in a while she met someone in real life that she really wanted to see in lingerie. Trial of the trade, she supposed. Benji was a good example. He looked flawless in the stuff she designed. Big and jacked and full of contradictions. From the moment they'd met, she had yearned to make lingerie for him.

She felt that same tug with Amanda.

She imagined Amanda in a piece from her decadent new collection of robes, dressing gowns, and peignoirs. Ultra luxurious. Super flirty.

But she had to stop sketching editorial photoshoots in her head and focus on the issues at hand. Which were not Amanda's measurements. Or the way her skin would glow if covered in black English net and marabou. Or, *oh*, what about that champagne charmeuse dressing gown with the—Nope. Wren needed to focus.

"About our cottage," she said, wrenching her mind

away from lingerie. "It's called the Chalet, but in the description, it's labeled as perfect for the junior executive. Did I tell you that?"

They came to a stop in front of the cottage door.

"No, you didn't."

"Right. I wasn't paying attention. I mean, *junior* and *executive* sound like nothing words to me." Wren used her keycard to open their cottage. They stepped inside.

The Chalet was a small two-story building with lots of windows, exposed wood, and a brick fireplace. The bottom floor had a sitting area, a lavish bathroom, and what Wren had expected to be a bedroom. Upstairs was a loft bedroom and another fireplace. There was also a private saltwater hot tub on the covered back porch, which was the type of extravagance Wren didn't know how to deal with now that she had money. She'd grown up swimming in a horse trough with the other kiddos in the trailer park, so a private hot tub was fanciness person-ified to her.

"This is gorgeous. Is that my room?" Amanda swung open the door. "Oh. Guess not."

There was a conference table in there. It had surprised Wren as well. It seemed so out of place. Evidently this was where they expected those junior exec-utives to make deals and influence people. Or whatever it was that businessy folks did. She was luckily successful enough that she could hire junior executives to do that job for her lingerie endeavors.

"William was the one who booked the reservations. The resort is courting him to take over one of the bars or be in charge of their event circuit. Or something. I don't pay attention," Wren said in a rush. "Either way, he had the hookup. I didn't look at pictures first. I'm so sorry."

Wren should have done her own research, but instead, she'd jumped in feet first without investigating. Then invited along a friend.

"It's fine." Amanda dropped her suitcase and a garment bag on the stone floor. Her eyes seemed panicky. "So, there's only one bedroom."

"Yes."

"And only …" Amanda touched her forehead and laughed.

"One bed. Yeah. Is that all right? I could sleep on the sofa." Wren turned toward the couch. It was more of a love seat, but she was short. She would make it work.

"No! Of course we can share a bed. That's not a big deal."

"You're sure?" Wren asked. Amanda was kind of acting like it was a big deal. Maybe she snored. Not that Wren would mind. Wren was a bit of a sleep cuddler, latching on to anything and anyone in her vicinity. Everyone had their flaws.

"Positive. It'll feel like a sleepover. We can talk about boys."

"And girls."

Amanda flushed and let loose a shy smile, which Wren wanted to eat right off her face. "Yes. Anyway …" Amanda dragged her bag into the bathroom with her. "Bye. See you soon."

Wren laughed and trudged upstairs with Amanda's

garment bag. This was going well. *Not.* They needed to find their footing again. Figure out how to translate their chatty, secret-spilling online life to face-to-face communication.

Wren found one of the fluffy resort robes that seemed to be everywhere and threw it on over her swimsuit. She would shower off the chlorine when Amanda was done. The bed in the loft was a queen with a modern wooden headboard and lots of pillows.

Wren pulled up the DMs between her and Amanda from a little over a week ago. In one, Amanda had said that she'd never had a fun New Year's Eve.

That moment had solidified it for Wren. She had decided to be an obnoxious, pushy pain in the hide until Amanda agreed to meet her here at Father Time Farm and Resort. Amanda deserved the best New Year's Eve, and Wren would give it to her.

Plus, Wren hadn't exactly been looking forward to watching Benji and William or her friends, Rosie and Leo, who were coming for the New Year's Eve party, suck face at midnight. With Amanda here, they would both be kissless, so it wouldn't feel so lonely.

But before Wren could give Amanda a rocking New Year's Eve, she had to figure out a way to get them over this awkwardness hump. She thumbed out a message to Amanda, even though she was only a few rooms away and in the shower.

Wren: *New plan.*

Wren: *Old year's resolutions (get it?). A bit of fun to end this orbit around the sun.*

A few minutes later, the shower shut off, and Wren's phone lit up with a new message.

Amanda: *Tell me more.*

Wren smiled. She enjoyed talking to Amanda like this. It was familiar.

Wren: *We have 2 days left of this year. Let's make simple, fun resolutions that we can fulfill before midnight on New Year's Eve.*

Wren: *We'll finish the year out with some successes.*

Amanda: *You're going to have to give me an example.*

Wren closed her eyes and let herself sink deeper into the pillows. It would be easy to write something like "meet someone interesting at the bar tonight." But Wren hadn't clawed her way to the top of the lingerie game by taking the easy road.

Wren: *Okay. Here's one. My first old year's resolution: Figure out how to ease the way with you in person so we don't feel like strangers. I'm greedy. I want both—online and in-person friendship.*

Wren listened as the bathroom door opened downstairs and footsteps fell on the staircase. Amanda slipped into the bedroom. She was wearing high-dollar skinny jeans and a retro patterned blouse with a tie at the neck. Her hair was wet, and her face was free of makeup. She lay down next to Wren, but rather than speaking, she typed a message into her phone.

Amanda: *I wanted to impress you, but then I fell into a pool. I'm scared you'll see the truth, which is that I'm not nearly as interesting when I can't proofread and labor over every word I say.*

Wren's heart lodged in her throat. Amanda had no idea how spectacular she was.

Wren: *I am impressed. No one has ever looked so good falling into a pool.*

Amanda laughed softly. It was oddly intimate to be carrying on a conversation without speaking out loud. To watch the play of emotions on Amanda's face as she read Wren's words. Wren imagined that this was how Amanda looked when they were texting, and regardless of what happened this New Year's Eve, Wren was going to cherish that image forever.

Wren started typing again, and Amanda seemed content to wait while she did.

Wren: *I know you're interesting.*

Wren: *You're one of the coolest people I've ever met.*

Wren: *You're creative. You're warm. You're clever. I already knew those things. Because I know you.*

Amanda: *Why is it easier to talk this way?*

Wren hooked their pinkies together on the bed between them. Amanda let out a shaky breath.

Wren: *Muscle memory. Just need to build up other muscles.*

Amanda smiled. She was typing on her phone with her right hand since Wren had commandeered her left, and it took her longer than usual. Wren wondered if Amanda was left-handed. She couldn't wait to find out all kinds of new things about her friend.

Amanda: *I don't feel like I'm any of those things. Cool, interesting, creative, etc. Or if I am, I'm not using those traits. My job is boring. I never do anything exciting or fun. I do what my family expects of me, which is show up, look pretty, and not make waves. Then I spend my free time in front of the TV or rage-scrolling through Twitter.*

Wren wished she knew how to help Amanda on the job front, but it was hard to detour out of the carefully crafted life you'd always known.

Wren: *Hey, Twitter brought us together, so I'm not gonna say anything negative about that.*

Amanda: *That's true.*

Wren: *Sometimes I wish I had a boring job I could turn off at 5 p.m. One that didn't take up so much of my emotional bandwidth.*

"But what you create is so beautiful. It's art." Amanda's voice made Wren jump. It was soft and close.

Wren rolled onto her side so she was fully facing Amanda. Amanda mirrored her. Their pinkies were still linked like a promise.

"One day, you're going to open the Disco Ball Bazaar —a vintage clothing store—and really stick it to your parents. I want a front-row seat," Wren said.

Amanda scrunched up her nose. She had freckles. They fanned out down the sides of her nose. Wren longed to touch them.

She refrained.

"I'd never call it that," Amanda said with a small huff. "It will be the Mothball Barn."

"That's a terrible name."

"What about Rusty Zipper Vintage and More?"

Wren laughed. "Better, but not great." She reached over and lightly fingered the bow of Amanda's blouse. "Where did you get this? It's cool."

"It was my godmother's when she was in high school."

"I love it."

Amanda bit her lip. "Me too."

Wren treasured the openness on Amanda's face. She'd known it would be awesome to be together in person, but she'd never expected Amanda to spill vulnerability all over the place right off the bat. Normally, Amanda was collected and wry. Wren liked seeing these new facets of her. The insecure and imperfect bits were perfect to Wren.

It was bravery, that was what it was. Amanda might have been forced to admit some shit because she'd tripped into a pool and was embarrassed, but it was still brave. Wren wasn't brave. Not brave enough to talk about the sadness she felt that everyone in her life was moving on and coupling up. Not brave enough to admit that she was scared she would never find a partner to take her seriously, to see past her messiness, or, better yet, love her for that chaos.

"What resolution are you going to make, Amanda? What's something we can work toward in the next, oh, three hours? Something *fun*."

Amanda's eyes sparkled in the low lights of the bedroom. They were a gorgeous blue. The blue of deep lake water and temptation.

"You first."

"We already resolved my old year's resolution. Don't you think?" Wren said. "If we have to lie side by side and text, I'm okay with that. It's nice being near you."

Everything about being in Amanda's presence was nice.

22

"Okay. A resolution. I want to … come out of the closet to you."

Wren tangled all their fingers together. "You've already done that, haven't you?" Amanda had shared very early on in their friendship.

"Yeah. But I've never told anyone in person, out loud. Just online."

That *was* news to Wren. She'd assumed Amanda didn't have much experience with people who weren't the cis men her mom had set her up with, but never even saying it out loud? Wren hoped she handled this right, that Amanda would see she was valued and loved.

"Okay. I'm here. Ears wide open."

Amanda smiled a full-blown smile, and a tiny dimple popped in her cheek. Wren felt like she'd discovered that dimple. Like she was on a treasure hunt, and that dimple was the prize at the end.

"Wren, I'm bisexual."

"Samesies. Wow."

A giggle fit overtook Amanda, and Wren watched in absolute delight as Amanda lost it.

"How did that feel?" Wren asked once Amanda had caught her breath.

"Amazing."

"Good. You deserve amazing. You *are* amazing." Wren gave her hand a squeeze and sat up. She felt breathless herself. "I'm going to shower off this chlorine. Be thinking about your next resolution."

Wren started to get off the bed. Amanda had an adrenaline-rush glow on her face, and she was so pretty.

And Wren was so happy for her. And so proud of her. And kind of ridiculously smitten.

Oh. No.

Wren leaned in and kissed Amanda's cheek. Which was a totally normal thing to do. *It was.* She kissed her friends on the cheek all the time. Hell, she kissed some of her friends on the lips. It wasn't weird, and it did not give her flutters or tingly fingertips. Not at all.

Chapter Three

Amanda felt high as she settled into a seat at the bar. She'd only been high once in her life, and she'd liked it, so she'd been very diligent about staying away from that feeling permanently. Lying in bed with Wren, sharing not-quite secrets, holding her hand, and getting a kiss on the cheek—it was like being high without the paranoia.

Nothing they had done was wrong. She knew it wasn't inherently romantic either. Just two friends being friends. But it had felt so good in all the ways Amanda wanted romance to feel good.

The bartender coughed, and Amanda snapped back to the present. They had gotten to the bar before William and Benji to "pregame," a concept Amanda had never participated in. Then Wren had forgotten her ID, so she'd had to run back to their cottage to get it.

"Decide what you want yet?" the bartender asked. "Need any help?"

Amanda was usually a vodka soda girl, but she was on vacation. She wanted to try something new.

"Which of these New Year's Eve cocktails would you recommend?" Amanda pointed at the menu.

A man who was sitting a few seats down said, "Her drink is on me."

Amanda frowned. "No, thank you. I can get my own." Though she was tempted to buy from the tippy-top shelf and leave him with the bill.

"It depends," the bartender said, ignoring the man. "Do you want something weird or classy?" She gave Amanda a cheeky smile, and Amanda did a double take. She was an attractive Black woman with a tattoo snaking up the side of her neck and mischievousness in her eyes.

"Weird."

"Sweet. I'd recommend the Melon Ball Drop Martini, then. It's neon green and has—"

"Neon sounds great. Thank you." She handed over her credit card so it was very evident she was paying for her own Melon Ball.

The guy scooted onto the barstool closest to Amanda. She glanced around for Wren or even Benji and William.

"I'm Hayden Worth." He said his name like she should recognize it. She had a lot of experience with people who thought their name carried special weight. That was how her grandfather said his name, how her father said his, so, to be honest, she wasn't impressed.

"Hi." She rotated in her seat, checking the entrance of the bar again. Still no Wren.

"I own the biggest party entertainment company in the Midwest—Worth Entertainment Group."

And she did not care. "Okay."

"We partner with Father Time Farm and Resort to throw the New Year's Eve party here. It's the event of the year. Let me buy you a drink, and I'll tell you about it. The tickets are hard to come by, but I have an in." He said this with a wink. She hated winkers.

"I already bought my own drink, and I have a ticket."

The man studied her, which never boded well. "You're very lovely, but I bet you would be prettier without all that makeup. You can't beat natural beauty."

"Ah. You're out of luck then." She pointed at herself. "Nothing natural about me. Fake hair. Full makeup. Fake tits. Fake tan. I like the way I look. You're terrible at negging. Zero out of ten."

A thunderstorm started brewing on his face, and something violent and ugly twisted his mouth. She had no idea what had come over her. She was never that assertive. Or mean.

It was freeing.

"Hi, *my love*." An arm slid around Amanda's waist. Wren's arm. Wren lightly nuzzled her ear, a move that probably seemed very intimate, and whispered, "I caught the end of that. You okay?"

Amanda nodded, relieved giddiness zinging through her. She'd seen movies where a dude rode in and pretended to be the heroine's boyfriend to scare off a dickhead. The fact that Wren was playing that part almost made her giggle with excitement. And Wren made a hot knight in shining armor with her dark, plum lipstick, gunmetal gray eyeshadow, a leather jacket, holey jeans, and combat boots.

"Hey, *honey*. I was just chatting with Brayden here," Amanda said, intentionally getting his name wrong.

He sneered. "Oh, I see. You're a—"

"Here's your drink," the bartender said loudly. She slid the Melon Ball Drop Martini, which was in fact very green, across the polished bar. Then, "You struck out, Hayden. Move along."

"Shut up, Daisy. Don't make me talk to your manager again," he said, venom in his voice. The bartender—Daisy, evidently—rolled her eyes.

William and Benji arrived at that moment, and the glare William gave Hayden could have stripped paint.

"Talk to whose manager?" William said. "Ah, Hayden Worth. You're … existing here. I see you've met my friends." He gestured to Amanda and Wren.

Hayden's face drained of color. "Yes. Nice to see you, Mr. O'Dare … I've, uh, got an important dinner meeting, so I can't stay to chat. I'm sure you under-stand." He stood and strode out of the bar, turning in the opposite direction of both restaurants on the premises.

Amanda laughed. "Oh my God, that was great."

"What a little worm," William said.

Wren put her head on Amanda's shoulder. "He was so scared of you, Willie."

"God, don't call me that."

"Habit," Wren said.

William laughed. "He knows I could make a play for his event contracts with the resort if I wanted to."

"Do you want to?" Benji asked.

"Maybe now."

"You all came to my rescue. Thank you," Amanda said.

Daisy, the bartender, placed menus in front of everyone and said, "You had it handled." She smiled at Amanda.

Wren dropped her arm and lifted her head off Amanda's shoulder. Amanda had liked the proprietary way Wren had touched her. She liked a lot about Wren, and it made this in-person friendship thing very complicated.

Amanda was still riding high at dinner. Wren's next old year's resolution was to have dessert first. Amanda had never done that. It wasn't *proper*, but she was doing it tonight. The blood-orange champagne crème brûlée was an amazing appetizer.

She was having trouble remembering why she'd been so worried about coming to this girls' getaway.

Awesome food. Awesome company. Awesome bedmate, or, uh, roommate?

"Amanda, what do you do again? Wren told me, but I forgot," Benji said.

Oh yeah. That was what she'd been worried about. She was boring, had been born with a silver spoon in her mouth, and hadn't done anything in her life of her own volition. Stupid disco balls.

Some of that happy, tipsy, fuzzy feeling vanished. "I'm a manager of sales for my family's company."

"What do you sell?" Benji asked.

"Bulk glassware. Like for fancy weddings or Hollywood award shows."

"Is it a big company? Are you a millionaire?" Benji asked.

"Benji," William said, his voice stern and scolding

Amanda waved William off. "It's okay. It is big, yes, but not as big as it used to be. And no. *I'm* not a millionaire." Everyone else in her family was.

Her family dynamics and the business were hard to explain. She'd come from money but had paid her own way since graduating from college—at her own insistence. She'd been handed a job at the company on a silver platter but didn't enjoy it. She did what was expected of her, including dating assholes her mother chose and attending philanthropic events.

Correction: she had done what was expected of her until this New Year's Eve trip when she'd thrown all that good daughter bullshit out the window. She might as well enjoy her time off the block.

"What did it used to be?" Benji asked. "Your family business?"

"A disco ball manufacturer. The largest in the US."

"Shut up! That is so cool."

"My coworkers call me the disco ball heiress behind my back. I hate it."

A stunned silence followed her words. Amanda could not believe she'd said that. She glanced down at her third Melon Ball Drop Martini. *Damn it.*

Wren, who knew all about Amanda's hatred of that

joke, squeezed her knee under the table, and it almost made that accidental slip worth it.

"Why do you hate it? You should own that. It's a fabulous fucking nickname," Benji said earnestly. He was leaning over the table, his shirt nearly touching his mashed potatoes. He was a few drinks deep as well.

Amanda laughed. "You think?"

"Yes! Get that shit tattooed on your body. William made me listen to a crime podcast where the murder weapon was a disco ball. They're dangerous and sparkly. You should own it."

William cleared his throat. "That was a lava lamp, babe."

"Oh. Shit. You're right." Benji slumped back in his chair.

"How did you two meet online?" William asked, changing the subject.

Wren moved her thumb slowly over Amanda's leg and said, "I tweeted about wanting a vintage lingerie pattern, and Amanda responded."

"I think your exact words were 'My kingdom for a '50s baby doll teddy pattern,'" Amanda said.

"Yes. And you sent me a picture of a pattern you owned and offered to send it for free, which was very stupid of you. They're worth good money."

Amanda bit her lip on a smile. "So you paid me for it, and I mailed it to you. And now you need to give me your kingdom. That's why I'm here. Time to pay up."

Wren was leaning toward her slightly, her pale skin

flushed and her short dark hair artfully messy. Amanda had never seen anyone prettier.

"Deal. I'll give it to you later." Wren blew her a kiss.

Amanda's cheeks hurt from smiling so hard. This girls' getaway was just what she needed before going back to her shallow, superficial life.

William laughed suddenly like he was surprised, and they all turned toward him.

"Sorry," he said. "Putting some puzzle pieces together in my brain. Ignore me."

The look he sent Wren had all kinds of subtext, but Amanda didn't know him well enough to read any of it.

Wren said, "Shut up, Willie."

He laughed again.

None of that made sense to Amanda, but she was too giddy and also maybe a bit too tipsy to care.

After dinner, William and Benji had decided to take a snowy evening stroll through the grounds to the apple orchard, which was the source of the Father Time Cider the resort and farm was famous for. The orchard was decorated with Christmas lights for a few more days, and it was a big draw for guests. Amanda's coat was still wet, so outdoor winter strolls were a huge *no* for her. She and Wren headed back to their cottage.

As they got ready for bed, Amanda wondered what a person's choice of sleepwear said about them. She wore silky stuff because it felt like cool water on her skin, but revealing her pajamas to Wren, who designed lingerie and had a whole page of sexy nighties on her website, was intimidating. What would Wren think about her silk shorts and shirt? That she was a prude who wore pricey matching sets? That she was boring and predictable?

Amanda had run her mind ragged before she'd said *fuck it*, put on her pajamas, and trudged upstairs to their bedroom.

Wren was sitting cross-legged in the center of the bed in plaid boxers and a baggy old T-shirt. The sight practically melted the silk off Amanda's body. She was in big, big trouble.

Wren grinned and lifted a large Father Time Cider bottle in the air when she spotted Amanda. Amanda could make out the swell of Wren's small breasts through the thin material of the T-shirt, which was advertising a 2009 5k Fun Run. There was a hole in the shoulder seam. The boxers and shirt hung loose on Wren's waifish frame

Wren wore old clothes to bed, and Amanda found that insanely hot.

Frankly, she just found Wren hot. It was an issue.

They sat opposite each other with the bottle of cider between them. Wren took a slug and passed it over. She had started a fire in the stone fireplace in the corner, so it was cozy and comfortable in the loft.

"Okay, girl talk time, right?" Wren asked.

Some of the tipsiness from dinner had worn off, and Amanda simply felt soft and hot inside.

"Sure."

"Me first."

"You first what?" Amanda said. She placed her lips on the bottle. It was warm from Wren's mouth.

"To ask questions."

"Okay. Shoot."

"What is it that you want most in the new year?"

"In what way?" Amanda wanted so many things. A fulfilling job or hobby. Good sex. More friends.

"Hmmm. Excellent question. Let's start with romance. How about in a relationship? You dated that boring Brad guy for two years, but you haven't seemed serious about anyone since. Your parents throw dates at you all the time, but what are *you* hoping for? What do *you* want the most?"

If Amanda were braver or drunker, she would lean in and kiss Wren. Crack a cheesy line like, "I want you the most."

But she wasn't brave. At all.

She'd dated Brad because he'd been "the right type of man for someone of her status" according to her mother. If lackluster kissing and one-sided pleasure was what she got dating the Brads of the world, then she wanted nothing to do with that anymore. She didn't want Brad. She didn't want Thatcher Aldridge or Ned Applebaum III. She was sick and fucking tired of the same old bullshit.

She was sick of not being brave.

Honesty was difficult, though. Especially when she had to say it out loud, when she wasn't given the veil of text messages and distance.

"I would like to be with someone who sees me as more than a trophy for their arm."

"*Yes.*" Wren flopped onto her side and pointed at Amanda. "You're more than your frankly fantastic looks, A."

"Frankly fantastic, huh?" When men complimented her, she always felt a bit irritated and distrustful. So often compliments were couched with desiring something from her—connections to the Ellis family business or nude pictures or money. It didn't feel that way with Wren, and she really liked it.

It made her wonder if any of the other things she'd learned to dislike would be better if the source were Wren.

"Yep. So what else?" Wren asked.

Recklessness flushed through her. There were things she thought about when she got off, but that she'd never been comfortable broaching with a partner. But Wren wasn't her partner. Wren was her friend. One of her very best friends.

She closed her eyes. "I want to be able to be honest and for my partner to listen." She'd slept with so many men who didn't see her as an individual, didn't take into account her desires, her preferences. "I want sex ... hot sex, that's like super dirty, but"—she took a big gulp of cider and wiped her hand over her lips—"I don't know how to get that without it being ugly. I don't want to choke on someone's dick or be used. I don't want to be called names but also kind of *do* want to be called names, you know? I want my dirty sex to be romantic, and I've yet to find anyone capable of that. It's either tedious as hell or demeaning."

Wren slipped the bottle out of Amanda's hand. Amanda opened her eyes in time to see Wren's lips come away from the bottle slightly wet.

Oh God.

"I understand what you want," Wren said, her voice indulgent and slippery in the near darkness.

Those might have been the hottest words ever spoken, and Amanda was pretty sure Wren wasn't even trying.

"You do?"

"Yeah. You want someone to call you a 'pretty little bitch' because it'll make you feel good, and they worship *you*. Not because they think you're actually a bitch."

Amanda nodded. Her heartbeat pulsed in her ears.

That was exactly it.

Bingo. A hole in one.

"You want to be held down and eaten out because you've been a good girl, and you deserve to be lavished with pleasure."

Amanda held her breath. She didn't know how to look away. Wren was watching her with intensity and calculation in her dark brown eyes.

"You want it to be a give and take between you and your partner," Wren said. "Not only a take. To find someone generous. To maybe be generous in return?"

"Uh-huh." Amanda's whole body felt hot and shaky.

God, she was turned on. Yeah, she'd been on a knife's edge all day because Wren just got to her, but this was something else. She couldn't remember the last time her motor had turned over so fast. She shifted, the silk of her sleep shorts sending a wave of sensation through her. She ached to have that silk on her clit. Her ass. Without the barrier of her panties.

"You want someone who can stuff you full without it feeling like they're taking from you. To press their fingers into your mouth because they love the feel of your tongue and you love the taste, not because they want to silence you."

"Yes." Amanda gasped in a noisy breath. "That."

Wren smiled like she knew exactly the effect she was having on Amanda. It seemed deliberately evil but in the best way. In the exact way Amanda craved. Wren was teasing her, and Amanda loved that, but if it wasn't real, she didn't think she could withstand more of it. Fuck, Wren could probably talk her into an orgasm without much effort. All Amanda had to do was shift and …

Amanda shot off the bed. "Need to pee. BRB."

She was halfway down the staircase before she realized she'd literally said "BRB" out loud.

The embarrassment should have been a douse of cold water, but it didn't even touch the heat spreading through her.

She reached the bathroom, shut and locked the door, and ripped down her shorts and panties. Luckily, she had the foresight to turn the water in the sink up to full blast because the moment she touched her clit, a low moan escaped her throat.

She was wet and blood warm, her heartbeat throbbing in her pussy. Fuck, it wouldn't take much, and it wouldn't take long. She planted a hand on the sink, spread her legs, and peered herself in the mirror.

Her hair was messy, spilling over her shoulders and down her back. Her eyes were bright, her cheeks red. Leaning over like this, she could see the top of her breasts through the loose neck of her sleep shirt. Her peaked nipples tented the silk.

This was reckless and wild and undoubtedly a mistake, but nothing was going to stop her.

She'd never felt so sexy, and that was Wren's doing. It was the thought of Wren sticking her fingers into Amanda's mouth or calling her a "pretty little bitch."

"Shit."

She caught her wetness on the tips of her fingers and circled her clit. If she were alone, if Wren wasn't upstairs looking hot and waiting for Amanda to come back, she would have drawn this out. Really worked herself up and lingered over the good thoughts and feelings bubbling inside her.

Instead, she moved her fingers fast over the hard, slick nub of her clit and stared as the flush of arousal spread down her cheeks and onto her neck until she was unable to keep her eyes open at all.

She came in a rush as silently as possible. Her knees trembled, and arousal slipped over her fingers, glossing the inside of her thighs in slow pulses.

"Goddamn."

It hadn't taken her longer than two minutes to get off, and she hoped it wasn't super obvious she'd been taking care of herself down here. Her blood was still thrumming sweetly, and she had a hard time making herself care.

Finally, the room stopped spinning. She cleaned herself up and prepared to head back upstairs. To sleep. In the same bed as Wren Rebello.

Chapter Four

Wren had screwed up. Or done something brilliant.

She wasn't sure which.

As soon as Amanda opened the door by talking about sex, Wren had gleefully skipped through it.

She hadn't preplanned it. The words had just spilled out.

Of course, then Amanda had bolted, and Wren had started to second-guess herself.

She'd been rash. Reckless. She'd dirty talked one of her best friends, a woman she hadn't met in person until today, without thinking through the repercussions first.

She was repeating past patterns rather than closing the door on bad habits. Not the finest way to commemorate the coming new year. Or … maybe … a last hurrah of bad habits was *exactly* the way to end the year.

Shoot. Making informed decisions was hard.

Screwing around with Amanda was not the best way to solidify a friendship or turn a crush into a relationship, but the devil in her brain was popping champagne and writing a toast.

Fuck, and now she was worked up. She ran her palm lightly over the front of her T-shirt and brushed against one of her nipples. Her pussy ached with the need to be touched, even though there would be no relief unless she grabbed a toy out of her bag.

Wren was not doing that. For one, Amanda might be back any second. She'd gone downstairs to jill off—*secretly*, but Wren wasn't born yesterday—and Wren had no idea how long that might take her.

Two, Wren loved the aching, the longing, the unresolved tension tightening her body.

The bathroom door opened and closed, and Wren heard Amanda's footsteps on the stairs.

Only a couple minutes. Impressive.

Wren was a slow cooker herself, especially without the help of something high-powered, so speed and receptiveness turned her on.

When Amanda reached the top of the stairs, she was a little flushed but otherwise very composed. Wren wanted to drag her down and make her messy again. Damn.

Not yet. Maybe not ever. Wren was notorious for making the let's-feel-good decisions rather than the smart ones. Maybe she needed to think through the smart decision in this instance.

"Are you sleepy?" Amanda asked. Her voice was raspy.

"Yeah. I'm ready to call it a night. You?" Hopefully, in the morning everything would be clearer.

Amanda smiled and climbed under the covers. She rolled so her back was facing Wren. That was good. Some distance.

Wren turned off the lamp and closed her eyes. She had to get a grip. They were friends, and they were not the type of friends who got each other off. Maybe with a bit of communication—communication that wasn't just dirty talk disguised as gossip—they would be able to take a step in that direction. Or maybe even step in the more-than-friends-with-benefits direction.

That was what Wren wanted. The possibility of more. They were not going to be able to broach that topic tonight, however.

Tomorrow. Tomorrow, they would come up with old year's resolutions. They would eat expensive food and drink pricey cider. They would indulge in saltwater hot tubbing. They would have fun like friends. Tomorrow would be a new day. One step closer to New Year's Eve.

One step closer to Amanda flying back to her life as a reluctant heiress half a country away.

Sleep started to pull Wren under. She let her mind drift to the breathing of the woman beside her. The heat of Amanda's body under the covers. The cinnamon-and-amber scent of Amanda's hair was the last thing on Wren's mind as she drifted off.

Some time later, Wren woke up with a jolt. The room was pitch black, and no light filtered through the window. The fire in the fireplace had burned out.

Silk skimmed over her legs.

No, not silk. Something better.

Warm, smooth skin hot from sleep.

Amanda's eyes were closed, and they were facing each other. Wren had a hand fisted over Amanda's hip, and their legs were twisted together. Amanda's hands were curled up against Wren's chest.

"Shit, shit, shit," Wren said under her breath.

She tried to disentangle their legs, but Amanda rolled closer and slotted her head under Wren's chin. Wren's senses went on high alert.

"Okay. This is okay," Wren whispered. And she couldn't help herself—she had to touch Amanda's hair, spread out behind her on the pillow. It was so soft and satiny under Wren's fingertips.

Suddenly, Amanda rubbed her nose against Wren's throat, and Wren had to stifle her own gasp.

Amanda's body, which had been lax with sleep, tensed. She murmured, "Wren?"

"Yep?" Wren's voice was threadbare.

"Oh." Amanda audibly swallowed, the sound like a gunshot in the quiet room. "I'm not normally cuddly. I'm sorry." She started to roll away, but Wren stopped her.

"I think it was me. I *am* cuddly."

Amanda's face was still hidden from Wren's view, and the darkness in the room was a veil, protecting them from pesky things like reality. The press of their bare arms and legs was heavenly, and Wren didn't want to think too hard about it. Didn't want to think hard enough to put a stop to it.

What Wren needed was a sign. If there was no sign, she would continue to lie there, buzzing with sleepy, dreamy yumminess. She would cuddle Amanda until they fell back asleep like the very good gal pals they were.

If there was a sign, though.

Oh, if there was a sign …

She didn't know what she would do, but it would probably be amazing. And a bad idea. But amazing.

Wren was breathing hard, her heart slamming in her chest. Amanda's breath matched hers, which was erotic in itself but not a sign.

Then Wren clocked an almost imperceptible sensation —Amanda's fingertip trailing down her spine.

Goosebumps broke out over Wren's skin. She moaned.

It was an accident, that moan. Soft and nearly silent.

But Amanda jolted. Then she echoed the sound. Her own voice tortured.

A sign.

Or close enough.

Wren jumped into action. It was what she did best. She fisted Amanda's hair and tilted her head back.

Amanda's lips parted. Wren kissed her like it was a question that Wren longed for Amanda to answer.

Amanda melted with a shaky breath as Wren feathered kisses along the seam of Amanda's mouth until she reached the middle of her plump bottom lip. Wren sucked gently, trying to get a small taste without pushing too hard.

"Okay?" Wren whispered.

Amanda nodded and pressed their lips together urgently. Her fists were clenched in the back of Wren's shirt, and her body was taut. She felt like untapped energy under Wren's hands.

Pent up. Amanda was pent up.

Wren continued to kiss her. A tender, soothing give and take. She coaxed Amanda to open her lips wider. Their tongues touched, velvety and hot and slow. Wren ran one hand lightly up and down Amanda's back and cupped her cheek with the other.

But Amanda didn't seem to want soothing or tender. She clutched at Wren and pressed against Wren's body. It made Wren itch to slow down more. To draw it out, make it sweet until Amanda was at a boiling point.

Amanda ripped her mouth away and took a few big, gulping breaths. Wren moved her lips to the hinge of Amanda's jaw, then the soft spot under her chin.

"Wren," Amanda breathed. She was trembling.

"Hmm?" Wren licked over her throat.

Amanda rolled to her back and took Wren with her. Wren's thigh landed between Amanda's legs, and she arched into it.

"Wren." This time her name was a moan.

Wren lifted her head and pressed up onto her hands so her weight wasn't on Amanda. "Yes?"

"*Yes.*"

"Oh." Wren let her gaze travel over Amanda's body in the dark. The dips and shadows, her heavy tits, her hair a halo around her head. Goddamn, but Amanda was gorgeous.

"Please," Amanda whispered.

They needed to talk. Needed to have a conversation using words rather than their tongues, but that was tomorrow's problem.

"Want to hear my next resolution?" Wren kneeled between Amanda's legs and rucked up her silky shirt to reveal her stomach.

"Uh-huh."

Wren kissed the skin above Amanda's belly button. Her body was supple and plush.

"Fall asleep with your taste on my lips."

"Then come up here and kiss me again."

"Oh, pretty girl." Wren nosed at her waistband. "Not that taste."

"Oh God."

Wren glanced up. She slid her hands slowly up Amanda's legs. "You like that resolution?"

"*Yes.*"

"Safety first. I was tested recently. All clear."

Amanda blinked as if she was coming out of a daze. "Yeah, same. Well, not recently. A few months ago, but I haven't been with anyone since."

"Good." Wren ripped Amanda's sleep shorts down. She was wearing a black cotton thong. Amanda lifted her hips, so Wren tugged that down too.

Wren grabbed Amanda's knees and parted her legs so they were spread wide. Amanda's cunt glistened, already wet, and Wren wished it was brighter in the room. In the dark, Amanda was a sight to behold. Amanda in the daylight would be a masterpiece.

"This is what's going to happen. You tell me yes or no, okay?" Wren said.

Amanda's breath was heaving, and she twisted her hips. "God, please, Wren. Whatever you want."

"What I want is to take you apart with my mouth, nice and quick. Real cookie-cutter shit because it's the middle of the night and you need your sleep. So I'm gonna suck on your clit until you come. Nothing crazy. Nothing wild. My mouth, your clit. Can you come that way?"

A shiver racked Amanda's body. "Yes. Please, Wren. I feel …"

"What do you feel?"

Amanda thrust her hands into her own hair and fisted it. She looked so fucking sexy.

"Like a cork that's about to pop. Please, Wren. Touch me."

Pent up. Untapped energy. *Mine.*

Amanda was Wren's, for the next few minutes at least, and Wren wasn't going to take that for granted.

"I will, Amanda. I'm going to get something for me, okay?"

Amanda nodded frantically, so Wren leapt off the bed and tore through her bag. She knew she had toys in there. She had a whole travel setup that permanently stayed in her toiletry bag, but she hadn't expected to need it during this girls' getaway.

Her hand hit the smooth head of a toy. *Yes.* A wand.

She pulled it out of its lint-free travel sack and dove back into bed. "Still with me?"

"Yes."

Wren went down onto one elbow and used her other hand to hold the wand between her own legs through her shorts. Then Wren spread Amanda's pussy lips wide and licked over her clit. Amanda let loose a sobbing moan. It sounded like pure relief and was enough to make Wren wet. She turned on her wand to a low setting and let the vibration flow through her.

Amanda tasted sharp and rich, her juices slicking everything up nicely. Wren wanted to delve inside her with fingers and tongue and toys and, damn, whatever she could fit, but that wasn't what they'd agreed on. Maybe next time. Or the time after that.

Fuck, all Wren wanted was an infinite number of times.

Wren sucked on Amanda's clit. She listened to Amanda's breathy noises, read the twisting and arching of her body until Wren was positive she was on the right track. She'd found the right rhythm, the right pressure.

Amanda's thighs tensed around Wren's head, so Wren pinned one of Amanda's legs to the bed, and Amanda shuddered underneath her.

"That's it, A," Wren rumbled against Amanda's cunt. She felt the telltale clenching of Amanda's muscles. Wren sucked hard on her clit. "Come on my lips like a good fucking girl."

"*Yes* ... Oh God." Amanda abruptly latched onto Wren's shoulder, her fingernails digging into the flesh through Wren's T-shirt. "Yes. Yes."

Amanda's clit pulsed on Wren's tongue. This was

Wren's favorite moment. Those few, eternity-long seconds when time and reality were suspended, and everything ached, and relief was only a breath away. She loved getting her partners there. Drawing it out. Making them scream or sigh or say her name.

Amanda didn't scream. Or sigh. But she sure as shit said Wren's name. Again and again as her orgasm throbbed through her, shook her like an earthquake, and drenched Wren's chin.

Wren didn't let up. She twirled her tongue around Amanda's clit until she was twitching and jerking from an overload of sensation.

And that quickly, Wren's own arousal became sharp and impossible to ignore. She shucked her shorts to midthigh, spread her legs as much as she could, ramped up the vibrator to ten, and moved to press her face back against Amanda's pussy. She was content to kiss at Amanda's pussy until she exploded, but Amanda had other plans.

She pushed against Wren's shoulder until Wren was kneeling upright. Amanda sat up so they were face to face, her legs splayed around Wren's knees.

Wren's mouth and chin were wet. Her face was hot. The vibrator was loud in the hushed stillness. Amanda stared at her. Watched her.

Without saying anything, Amanda leaned in and licked delicately over Wren's chin.

"Yeah, baby," Wren breathed. She threaded her fingers into Amanda's long hair and cupped the back of her head.

"Can I touch you?" Amanda whispered. She seemed innocent and curious, and Wren about came on the spot.

Wren nodded, the ability to speak leaving her the closer she got to orgasm. The room was blurring around her.

Amanda dipped her hand below the vibrator and strummed her fingers through Wren's swollen folds. She didn't push inside, just played with Wren's labia. That gentle touch coupled with the intense vibration on her clit was a clash of opposing forces, both strong and perfect in their own right, but better mingled together.

Wren kissed Amanda hard, delving her tongue deep into Amanda's mouth and stroking. Amanda was pliant and soft. Giving.

The hot, hollow ache in the small of Wren's back contracted, then bloomed out to her core, to her clit. She ripped her mouth away from Amanda's. She was gripping the side of Amanda's face with her free hand, probably holding on too hard, holding herself up, but she couldn't help it.

Amanda turned her head and sucked Wren's thumb into her mouth. And that did it. The end.

A wave of sensation flooded her nervous system, and she flew.

Chapter Five

Amanda woke up with a smile on her face. She was wrapped up tight in Wren's arms, and she felt good. Satisfied, but aching for more.

This was exactly what she needed. An escape. A few days away from her routine. A few days away from being the disco ball heiress. She would take this—whatever *this* was with Wren—and she wouldn't overthink it. She wouldn't analyze it to death. She would enjoy it because it was awesome, and she didn't know when she'd get something awesome again.

She would take a page out of Wren's playbook. Wren didn't seem to have trouble jumping into, well, trouble.

Wren shifted and hummed sleepily.

"Morning," Amanda said.

"Oh. Hi." Wren's voice sounded funny.

Amanda rolled over. "I want strawberries for breakfast. And champagne. And chocolate." Normally, she ate plain Greek yogurt and a granola bar.

Wren blinked a few times before laughing. "Okay. We can order room service."

"Yes! *That*."

"Are you always so perky in the morning?" Wren asked. That weirdness was back in her voice. If Amanda didn't know better, she would think it was shyness. Or uncertainty.

"No. But I'm …"

"What?"

"Excited to spend the day with you."

Wren's expression softened. "Me too."

"I'm going to order. Any preferences?"

"Nope."

"Great. I'll put it on my gold card." Amanda waggled her eyebrows, drawing another laugh out of Wren.

Amanda jumped out of bed and put in the most ridiculous and decadent order she could think of. Then she brushed her teeth because it was suddenly very important to her to have fresh breath. While she was in the bathroom, she decided to put on a little makeup—foundation, blush, mascara, lip tint—because it made her feel pretty. And she wanted to feel pretty for Wren. Her hair was slightly messy, but in a sexy way. Wavy and full and falling in billows past the middle of her back. She finger-combed it but otherwise left it alone.

Her stomach was all bubbly and jumpy. She had never been much of a giggler, but this morning, she could hardly conceal it.

Oh God. She had a *crush*. That was what those feelings were. A crush. A full-blown, please-pay-attention-to-me, pussy-throbbing crush.

When the room service arrived, Amanda rushed out of the bathroom to answer the door. An attractive young guy wheeled it in. There was more snow on the ground this morning than there had been last night. She tipped him extra for making the trek to their cottage. He smiled bashfully but wouldn't meet her eyes. Amanda closed the door behind him.

"You bamboozled him."

Wren's voice made her jump. Amanda spun around to find Wren standing at the base of the stairs.

"How so?"

"By looking like a sexpot, I'd bet." Wren's eyes raked over her, and a flush of heat spread through Amanda's chest.

"Breakfast is here."

"I see that. I'm going to brush my teeth. I'll be right back."

"Sure."

Amanda wondered if Wren was brushing her teeth for the same reason Amanda had. Hygiene ... but also kissing.

Damn, Amanda could not wait for more kissing.

Wren reappeared as Amanda finished laying out the spread on the coffee table between the loveseat and fireplace.

There was champagne, orange juice, a fruit platter, warm chocolate dipping sauce, croissants, mini waffles with petite pots of syrup, blueberry muffins, and glazed donuts.

"Holy shit," Wren said. "This is my dream breakfast. All these glorious carbs."

Amanda grinned. She knew Wren had a sweet tooth, and she'd picked accordingly. She wiggled the cork out of the champagne bottle. "Want some?"

"Hell yeah."

Amanda passed over a flute of champagne. Wren took it, filled a plate with baked goods, and lounged back on the couch. Amanda covered her plate in fruit and drizzled the chocolate over it.

They ate in silence for a few minutes before Wren blurted out, "Do we need to talk about last night?"

Amanda froze with a strawberry halfway to her mouth. "We can." She didn't really like the doom and gloom on Wren's face, though.

Last night had been a whole buffet of firsts for Amanda, but she didn't want to make a big deal of it. Amanda wasn't vibrating with excitement this morning because she'd finally kissed a woman. She was excited because that woman had been Wren.

Wren scratched at her bare knee. They were both still in their pajamas, and Wren looked as tasty as the blueberry muffins.

"I don't know," Wren moaned. "Talking is the responsible thing. I would like to be more responsible. I don't want to be the girl who doesn't take shit seriously, and I have no idea what you want or if you're okay. And—"

"Do I not seem okay?" Amanda asked.

"You aren't reacting the way I expected."

"What did you expect?"

Wren shot her a slightly guilty pout. "For you to freak out and overthink it."

"That does sound like me." Amanda smiled a little.

Wren threw up her hands, almost spilling champagne. "I know! I know you. But that's not what you're doing. Why not?"

Amanda ate her strawberry. "I'm happy. I'm on vacation, so there's a bit of unreality to the whole thing. Like consequences don't exist. And … I've always respected your ability to live in the moment. I want to live in the moment. I want to have *fun*, Wren."

"You're going to be rash and act without a plan or regard to consequences? You're *me* in this scenario?"

"I guess." Amanda smiled wider. "Is that okay with you?"

Wren hesitated, and Amanda started to worry that she'd read this whole situation wrong. Then Wren chugged a few gulps of champagne. "Okay, so you don't need a long, drawn-out conversation about what this means?"

"No. As long as our friendship is fine, I'm fine."

"And you want to keep fooling around until you go back to California on New Year's Day?" Wren asked.

"Yes."

Wren scrubbed her hands through her hair and laughed.

"What?" Amanda said.

"Nothing." Wren smiled and shook her head ruefully.

"I'm down to fuck, Amanda. So down it's not even funny. Just update me if there's anything I'm not giving you. Especially if it's emotional."

Amanda was oddly touched. None of her previous partners had asked for her to keep them apprised of her emotions, and she hated to admit it, but she'd expected her past boyfriends to figure out her feelings on their own. Maybe that wasn't fair to them. Maybe she needed to be open rather than expecting her partners to know her innermost thoughts by osmosis.

"Of course. Will you do the same?"

"I'll try."

That was all Amanda could ask for. She leaned back on the sofa, her plate in her lap and champagne in her hand. She was incredibly thankful that she'd ditched her parents' fancy party to be here.

"God, look at you," Wren said a few minutes later.

"What?"

"Yesterday, when we were walking down to our cottage after you fell in the pool, all I could think about was making lingerie for you. I would love to see you in this black-and-gold peignoir I brought to show Benji. Sitting there eating strawberries and drinking champagne at ten in the morning. Fuck me, Amanda. For real."

It took Amanda a second to parse that. "You want me to put on lingerie for you?"

"No, I want to *give* you a dressing gown."

Amanda followed Wren's professional accounts. Most of Wren's designs were modern, strappy, and badass. It was the type of stuff Amanda imagined hot people wore at sex clubs, but it never quite fit her style or comfort level.

She was doing lots of things out of the ordinary for her this New Year's, though.

"Okay."

"Really?" Wren said, surprised.

"Yes. I'm sure it's gorgeous."

Wren was off the sofa like a bullet. She ran upstairs and returned with a parcel wrapped in delicate tissue paper.

"Here." Wren handed it over.

Amanda unfolded the tissue paper to find the softest, filmy black fabric. It had long sleeves that belled out at the end and gold, feather trim. Amanda stood up and shook the garment out so she could see the whole thing. There was a gold silk tie at the waist and the same feather trim at the bottom. It was very retro, almost old Hollywood.

While most of Wren's lingerie creations didn't fit Amanda's style, this was different. More of a throwback. More indulgent.

"It's beautiful."

"Put it on," Wren said, her voice husky.

Amanda nodded. She gently set the robe down, then went about pulling off her pajama top.

Wren sat up abruptly when she seemed to realize Amanda was taking off her clothes. Amanda didn't think the robe would fit as well with her pajamas on underneath. She turned her back on Wren as she finished undressing, feeling shy. When she slid her shorts down her legs, leaving her black thong on, Wren groaned, the noise sending heat to Amanda's pussy.

She slipped the robe over her shoulders. The sheer material was so luxurious on her skin. She tied it at her waist, loving the way it cinched in and accentuated her figure. The feathers swept over her fingers and the floor. The robe even had a short train. She smoothed her hands down the front. The fabric ruched up and clung to her breasts. She could barely see her nipples peeking through the see-through fabric.

"Are you gonna turn around?" Wren asked from behind her.

Amanda rotated slowly. "How do I look?"

Wren's eyes went wide, and her pale cheeks went rosy pink. "Like it was made for you."

"It feels like it was. I would live in this if I could."

"You'd cause car crashes. People would walk into traffic. Men would swallow their tongues," Wren teased. "It would be awesome." Her gaze was intense, eating Amanda up slowly, lingering over every inch.

Finally, Wren met Amanda's eyes. There was lust and something more intense there. Something fragile. Wren blinked, and that fragile thread between them seemed to break. Amanda sat down on the sofa, spreading the dressing gown out around her.

Wren handed Amanda her plate of fruit. "Here. Watching you eat strawberries in that is going to fry my brain, but please do it."

Amanda laughed. "Seeing you in a swimsuit fried my

brain yesterday. At least there aren't any pools for you to walk into."

Wren dropped the muffin she'd been bringing to her mouth. "What?"

"Yeah. You were in that simple black two-piece. It surprised me. I couldn't take my eyes off you."

"Oh, Amanda, flattery will get you everything. Be careful, or I'll turn this breakfast into sex."

"I'm not opposed to that." Amanda tried to shrug, feigning nonchalance, but sex with Wren was the last thing she was nonchalant about. She wanted it really bad.

"Not yet. Let's talk. And eat."

"Okay …" Amanda took a sip of champagne. "Last night you asked what I wanted most in the new year, romance-wise."

"Uh-huh."

"What do you want most?"

Wren bit her lip, some of that shyness sneaking back into her expression. "To be taken seriously. I'm tired of being given up for lost because I'm wild or because I like to dance or because—"

"You're fun."

"Yeah." Wren smiled. "I don't want a run-of-the-mill life. I like going to barbecues that turn into orgies. I like getting rowdy with the roller derby team after practice. I like playing spin the bottle and going on last-minute vacations. I like smoking pot, and skinny dipping, and experiencing what life has to offer, but that doesn't mean I wouldn't be the best fucking wife in the world."

"You deserve someone who appreciates all of that about you."

"Yes. Please point me in the direction of this mythical creature or creatures."

"They are out there." A tiny seed of longing tried to bloom in Amanda. She was tempted to offer herself on a platter. To say, *Call me a unicorn because I can be that mythical creature*. Those traits Wren had been made to feel bad about were the exact reasons Amanda was here. She admired Wren's ability to have fun and let loose and *live*. Amanda wanted that in her life. Those traits were the exact reasons Amanda would be in trouble if she let her heart run free where Wren Rebello was concerned.

Luckily, they had agreed this was going to be uncomplicated and friendly vacation sex. A way to blow off steam at the end of the year. Amanda wasn't going to ruin that by getting mushy.

"I want to have a good time," Wren said, totally unaware of Amanda's mini crisis. "I don't want to be seen as a good time. You feel me?"

There was a surprising amount of pain in Wren's voice, even though she was smiling.

"I do." Amanda grabbed Wren's hand and tugged her closer. Wren came willingly, and that thrilled Amanda. "One day, you're going to find a partner, or partners, who sees what I see. What all your friends who love you see."

"What's that?" Wren asked, her voice catching.

A sudden trilling chime made them jump apart. Amanda glanced around dazedly, trying to locate the noise. Wren spotted it first—Amanda's ringing phone.

Wren picked it up and handed it to Amanda, but her thumb slipped over the screen, accidentally answering the call, which happened to be a FaceTime call.

Amanda's mother's face filled the screen, which was the shittiest luck. She was impeccably coiffed and wearing a fashionable but not showy blush blazer.

"Amanda, when should I send the dress by your apartment for tomorrow night's charity ball?" her mother asked without saying hello. "I'm sure you'd prefer to wear one of those silly vintage things you love, but this dress is much more appropriate than anything you would pick out."

"Mom."

"I've also selected heels for you. They match perfectly. Thatcher will love them."

"Thatcher?" Wren mouthed, and Amanda rolled her eyes.

"Mom," Amanda said again. "I texted you about this. I'm not—"

"Amanda, what in the world are you wearing?"

Amanda's stomach dropped. Nothing below her collarbones was visible on the screen, but her mom could clearly see the sheer fabric wrapping over Amanda's shoulders. That tone of voice haunted Amanda.

"It's a, uh …"

"Peignoir," Wren added helpfully from the other side of the room. Amanda loved the way the word peignoir rolled over Wren's lips.

"Whose voice was that? Where are you?" her mom asked.

"Mom, I told you a few days ago that I made other plans for New Year's Eve."

One of her mom's flawlessly shaped eyebrows arched. "Well, of course I didn't take you seriously. I told you that you needed to be there."

Yes, and Amanda always did what she was told.

Not this time.

"I'm sorry. I'm not even in California. I won't be there."

Her mom sniffed. "I just don't know what this means. What about Thatcher Aldridge?"

"I already sent him my regrets," Amanda said.

"Amanda Brittany Ellis, how rude. What if he doesn't have time to find another date? Oh no. What if he doesn't come to the charity ball at all?"

"That would not be the end of the world. He's a dick."

"Watch your mouth, missy." Her mom closed her eyes like she was trying to compose herself, and Amanda's fingertips started to tingle. She never talked back or did anything to disappoint her parents. It was at once thrilling and horrifying.

After an extended beat, her mom opened her eyes. "When will you be home?"

"I fly back on New Year's Day."

"I can find you a flight home today. I'll pay for it."

"No."

Her mom blinked. "No?"

Amanda was breathing hard. "No. I'll be home in a

few days. I'll deal with the fallout and your displeasure then."

"Very well." Her mom stared at her for five seconds. Amanda counted in her head, waiting for the ball to drop.

It didn't. Instead, the line went dead, and Amanda tossed her phone onto the couch cushion next to her.

"Oh my God." She laughed and covered her mouth with her hand.

Wren was standing opposite of her by the mammoth stone fireplace. She grinned and took off her T-shirt.

Chapter Six

Wren wanted to cheer. She knew that it was difficult for Amanda to stand up to her mother, but she'd done it.

That called for some celebratory bad behavior.

Amanda's mouth was open like she'd never seen a half-naked lady before.

Wren grinned and pointed out the large window. "Do you see those trees?"

Amanda nodded, evidently struck silent.

"They're my next old year's resolution."

"I don't understand," Amanda choked out.

"I'll race ya to 'em," Wren said, her childhood drawl sneaking into her voice.

"What?"

"Yeah. Take off the peignoir. Or leave it on. It's see-through anyway, so it counts."

"I, umm … I don't understand."

"Come on, pretty girl. We're going streaking."

An array of emotions passed over Amanda's face,

from disbelief to fear, but her expression ended on thrilled.

"Yes?" Wren asked. Her insides were still all jumbled from their interrupted conversation. She'd poured out her heart for Amanda to see, and Amanda had accepted it like it was precious.

But Wren didn't know if she could trust it. Her last major heartbreak had happened because her partners—a married couple—had moved away. They didn't think it was serious enough to try long distance with Wren. They'd told Wren that they didn't want to stifle her fun and carefree spirit by tying her down to something so difficult. They'd thought she was too wild and silly to even try.

Now, Amanda was telling her she wanted the live-in-the-moment Wren. The rowdy Wren, the Wren who had been rejected over and over again. And Wren was going to give it to her, but she was going to protect her heart too because she wasn't a dumbass.

This was a vacation hookup. A tiny drop in the bucket of time before Amanda went back to being the perfect daughter and heiress, hopefully armed with a little grit to stand up for herself.

Amanda stood and untied the peignoir, letting it fall open and loose around her breasts.

"God, you're so hot like that," Wren said, unable to help herself. "Leave that on while we run."

"What if someone sees us?"

"They won't." Wren had walked around before Amanda had arrived yesterday. Those trees were just beyond the back porch with the hot tub, which was definitely designed with privacy in mind. There was no reason anyone would be back there.

"It'll be cold."

"Yep. You in?"

A slow smile tripped over Amanda's gorgeous lips. She took a deep breath, then spun on her heels and sprinted to the back door. Wren laughed and ran to catch up with her.

The back door led to the enclosed back porch, where there was another door and two steps to reach the ground. Amanda made it outside first. She hitched the skirt of the peignoir up over her elbows and glanced back over her shoulder as Wren made it down the steps.

The cold hit Wren like a sledgehammer. The breath left her lungs, and she gasped out, "Oh my fucking fuck!"

Goosebumps sprouted up all over her body as her bare feet hit the snow. She covered her boobs with her hands out of instinct because it was freezing, but her hands were little ice cubes, so she dropped them.

Amanda turned and jogged backwards, laughing like she was having the time of her life. The cold had turned her cheeks bright red, and her bare tits bounced as she moved.

Wren wished she could spend an eternity tracing Amanda's tight nipples with her gaze, but it was too fucking cold to linger. This was an amazing idea, and it needed to be over ASAP. Wren took off toward the trees, and Amanda matched her stride. Their fingers brushed the branches of a blue spruce at the edge of the forest at the same time, and they seemed to turn back to the cottage as one.

Wren slipped when they were about twenty feet from the back door, and Amanda caught her wrist, managing to right her. Then they were running, breathless, with their hands locked. The day was as fresh as new snow. Full of infinite hope and opportunity.

They tumbled into the enclosed back porch, and Wren rushed to the hot tub. She slung the cover off, jumped in without taking her boxers off, and dunked her head to warm up her frozen ears.

Amanda slipped the peignoir off her shoulders and folded it over a chair with extra care even though she was hardcore shivering. She also took her thong off, so as she slipped into the hot tub, she looked like a naked winter goddess.

"Oh my god. It's so nice," Amanda groaned. She pulled a ponytail holder off her wrist and twisted her hair up into a messy bun. The steam licked around her cheeks and immediately curled the fine hair around her ears and temples.

"Yes." Wren swanned across the hot tub until she was in Amanda's space.

"That was the most fun I've ever had," Amanda said, her voice hushed.

"Good."

Amanda grabbed Wren by the back of the neck and yanked her closer. So close their lips touched.

It had been wonderful in the middle of the night, but this was better.

Amanda controlled the kiss, sucking sweetly on Wren's lips and turning her head just right to slip her tongue into Wren's mouth.

"Oh," Wren gasped and pressed closer, straddling Amanda's lap.

Their wet naked skin melted together in the hot water. Amanda cupped one of Wren's small tits.

"I didn't expect the piercings when you took your shirt off earlier," Amanda said, gently tugging the barbell shining in one of Wren's nipples. That tug went straight to Wren's clit. Amanda lifted Wren's body until her breasts were all the way out of the water. "We should have gotten naked last night. Does this feel good?"

"*Yes*." Wren arched into Amanda's touch and dropped her head back.

"I love boobs," Amanda mumbled against the soft slope of Wren's breast.

Wren laughed. "Yeah. They're great. You've got a rocking pair."

"They're fake."

"I know. Still awesome."

Amanda's arms tightened around Wren's waist. "Thank you. Can I use my mouth on your piercings?" Amanda asked.

"Yes. Gentle, though."

"Always." There was a smile in Amanda's voice that made Wren laugh.

"You don't *always* have to be gentle with me. My clit likes it … oh fuck me, *yes*."

Amanda ran her tongue lightly around Wren's nipple,

catching on the balls at the end of the bar. Her warm tongue, the steaming water, and the cold air outside the hot tub scrambled Wren's synapses, her nerves on high alert.

"How does your clit like it?" Amanda asked. That should have sounded dirty, but it didn't. It sounded like innocent interest, which made it infinitely hotter.

"Rough." Wren's eyes rolled back as Amanda moved to her other nipple. "And I usually need a vibrator to come."

Amanda released Wren's nipple with a *pop*, and Wren glanced down at her. Amanda's lips were wet and red.

"Good thing you brought a vibrator with you, then."

"Oh, baby, I have more than one. Designing lingerie for a popular sex toy company has its perks." Wren had been releasing exclusive lines of lingerie for Lady Robin's Intimate Implements for several years, and her friend Robin, the owner, regularly hooked her up with the goods.

"What else do you have?"

"A butt plug." Wren pecked Amanda on the lips. "A Monster Me dildo that's supposed to look like Shrek's dick." Wren leaned in to kiss Amanda harder, but Amanda sputtered with laughter, so Wren redirected her lips to Amanda's ears, to her neck, her shoulder.

Amanda went pliant under Wren's ministrations. Wren sat her butt on Amanda's thighs. Their torsos heaved together, both of them breathing hard.

Amanda's hands explored Wren's back, fingertips pressing hard against her spine when Wren fondled

Amanda's breasts, and harder when Wren slid her fingers down Amanda's stomach and dipped them to Amanda's cunt.

"Why don't I make you come in this hot tub, then we can take this party to the bedroom where my toys are, and you can return the favor?"

"Okay."

Wren smiled and swung off Amanda's lap. She gestured to the far side of the hot tub, the side that over-looked the forest they'd streaked to. "Go lean your chest over the edge with your butt out of the water. You should be able to kneel up on the seat."

Amanda blinked in surprise. "Oh. Umm."

"Do you trust me?"

Amanda nodded vigorously. "So much."

That shouldn't have felt so amazing, but it did. They were friends, which, of course, brought trust. But this was different. Sex was different. Sex was vulnerable and exposing. It highlighted secrets and desires. It opened you up and relied on you letting go. Wren was able to separate her internal baggage and feelings from sex if needed, but there would be no separation when it came to Amanda.

They'd already fooled around, but here in the daylight with eyes wide open, they were taking a bigger, more important leap.

"I'm going to make you come so hard you scream." Wren bit Amanda's bottom lip. "Get over there."

Amanda smiled. "Thank you for being so fun." She kissed Wren's cheek and moved to the other side of the hot tub.

There was that word again. *Fun.*

Wren adored bringing fun to Amanda's life even if Wren wanted it to be deeper. Fun would hold her over for now.

Amanda kneeled on the seat of the hot tub, facing out, and pressed her elbows to the wooden deck around the outside of it. Every part of her was out of the water except her thighs, knees, calves, and feet.

It should have been cold, but it wasn't. She was burning up.

She heard a splash as Wren moved up behind her. This position made Amanda feel particularly vulnerable and on display. Even more so when Wren strong-armed Amanda's legs farther apart, opening her up for Wren's eyes.

Any other time Amanda had been laid out on elbows and knees, it had been for uninspiring doggy-style. She knew that wasn't what Wren had in store for her.

The anticipation tightened Amanda's muscles. It took every ounce of her willpower not to stick her ass in Wren's face as Wren's breath ghosted over the inside of her thigh.

Water sluiced down Amanda's back, droplets slipping over all her most sensitive skin. Wren gripped Amanda's ass cheeks with her wet hands and spread her farther apart.

Amanda realized she would let Wren do anything she

wanted. She trusted her implicitly. She knew everything Wren did to her body was to make Amanda feel good.

An achy eagerness rippled through Amanda's pussy, and when Wren placed a kiss over Amanda's clit, Amanda's elbows almost gave out. Wren's mouth was so warm. Hotter than the water in the hot tub.

Wren's nose rubbed through her folds as she licked over Amanda's clit, and it was so dirty. Amanda had never experienced oral in this position. It felt extra naughty.

Last night had been quick and dreamy. Today, Amanda's need had been cranked up to eleven.

Wren squeezed her butt and jiggled it a little, making Amanda squirm.

"You have a gorgeous ass, A," Wren whispered, her voice dark and seductive and right up against Amanda's pussy.

Amanda pushed her ass into Wren's hands and was rewarded by a hard suck on her clit and a light slap on her ass. Wren spanked her again before gripping her ass, her thumbs near Amanda's hole.

Wren licked up through Amanda's pussy to her clit. She repeated this over and over again, all the while massaging Amanda's ass cheeks. Without warning, Wren let go and drenched Amanda's back with hot water from her cupped hands, heating Amanda's skin and sending a spiral of sensations ricocheting through her.

"Don't want you to get cold," Wren murmured, returning to Amanda's pussy. This time, Wren's thumbs edged Amanda's asshole.

"Jesus. Thank you."

"You like that?" Wren lightly circled Amanda's hole with her thumb.

"Y-y-*yes*," Amanda gasped out.

"That's my dirty girl." Wren rubbed her chin through Amanda's folds. "You wanna know what I love about your cunt?"

Wren paused as if she was waiting for a response, and Amanda managed to say, "Uh-huh."

"You get *wet*. Like dripping. It's so fucking sexy the way you soaked my face when you came last night. I want you all the fuck over me."

Amanda's body evidently loved hearing that because a rush of arousal slowly slicked down her thigh. Wren stroked her thumb through that slickness and put it right back at Amanda's asshole, pressing a bit harder this time.

"Oh my God!" Amanda thunked her head down onto the wooden deck and undulated toward Wren's hand. She hadn't realized that could feel so good.

The tip of Wren's thumb slipped inside, and Amanda whined when Wren pulled it back. Wren was no longer licking Amanda's clit, but her clit throbbed all the same.

The word "more" ripped out of Amanda's throat before it had registered in her mind. Usually, it would have embarrassed her, but there was no room for embarrassment here. Just passion and sharp-sided need.

"What do you want, Amanda?" Wren ran her tongue from Amanda's clit to her taint, over and over, teasing Amanda but never quite finishing the circuit. Never quite putting her mouth where Amanda craved it most.

"Wren," Amanda whined. Wren wiggled her thumb slightly deeper. "Please."

"Please *what*, pretty girl? You want to be bad?"

"Yes." Amanda's breath was leaving her in gasps, her chest heaving. Her body was trembling.

"Gotta say it." Wren nipped the fleshy part of Amanda's butt cheek. "It will turn me on to hear you ask for it. It can be one of your resolutions."

"Please, your mouth …"

Wren ran her lips over Amanda's pussy. "Yes?"

A shiver racked Amanda's body, and sweat trailed down her temple. She moaned. "My ass, please, Wren."

"Mmmm. My pleasure."

The first lick over Amanda's hole was a shock. She gasped and pushed up onto her hands, arching her back. For one incandescent second, she wondered if she looked like a mermaid coming out of the water, but then all thoughts left her completely. A whiteout in her brain. She was nothing but sensation. She felt nothing but Wren's wet, insistent tongue and blunt thumb pushing deeper.

The water from the hot tub lapped at her thighs, creating mini waves from Wren's movements. Amanda hardly noticed Wren's fingers on her clit at first, too flabbergasted by Wren's mouth. Then Wren lightly pinched the nub, rolling it hard between her fingers and thumb.

It was all too much. Her body was on overload. Those feelings had nowhere to go. Her muscles kept clenching, tighter and tighter.

And Wren wasn't shy. She played Amanda's body like a fiddle.

A fiddle she wanted to make scream.

When Amanda's orgasm finally hit her, she nearly shook apart. She definitely screamed. And she had no idea how she would ever give this up. How she would give Wren Rebello up.

She couldn't think about that right now. Nope. Not yet.

Instead, she put all her focus into returning the favor.

It didn't take them long to make it to the bedroom. Wren didn't even dry off, just followed Amanda as she raced upstairs.

"Do you need a toy?" Amanda asked.

"Yes." Wren tore through her toiletry bag and came up with a little thing that fit snugly over Amanda's index finger. "The Fingerslip. It's a vibrator."

Amanda felt almost frantic. Her blood was still pumping fast, and she needed Wren to feel the same way. Wren's eyes were wild as she shucked her wet boxers off, flopped back onto the bed, and spread her legs.

She had a landing strip of dark hair, and her pussy was rosy and plump with arousal. She was so fucking gorgeous.

There was a tattoo on the inside of her thigh very close to her groin that Amanda hadn't noticed when Wren had been in her swimsuit. It said *Stitch Bitch* in an embroidery font.

Amanda traced it with a fingertip. "When did you get this?"

"Last year. I thought about sending you a picture after

75

it was done but felt weird sending a picture of my crotch."

"It's your roller derby name, right?" Amanda said, and Wren nodded.

"A bunch of the team got them together. It was my idea," Wren admitted. "We weren't sober, but I like it."

Amanda pressed her lips to the tattoo. "I like it too." This close, she could smell Wren's pussy. It was intoxicating. "I've never done this before."

"It's okay." Wren tucked a tendril of hair behind Amanda's ear. A tender place in Amanda's chest twisted. "You don't have to do anything you don't want to."

"I want to." The words were so simple, but they seemed to hold the key to the fluttering in her chest. Amanda *wanted* to. There were so many things she wanted to experience. So many *wants*, but this was at the top of the list. "Tell me if I do it wrong."

Wren sucked in a shuddery breath. "All right."

Amanda tentatively licked up through Wren's pussy, slipping slightly inside, before reaching her clit. Wren gasped and fisted the bedspread underneath her. She was wet, both from being turned on and from being in the hot tub.

Amanda hadn't known what to expect. She'd tasted herself before. Had licked her fingers after making herself come and imagined what it would be like for that slickness to be someone else's. But Wren tasted different. Earthy and mellow on her tongue.

Amanda tasted again and again, loving it and thirsting for more. Wren gasped and let loose soft kitten sounds that were so different than the other noises Amanda had heard from her.

Amanda had been so sure that she knew herself. That she understood the depths of her desire, the shape that it could take. But this—the sex in the hot tub followed by Wren writhing on her lips—opened the door to a hunger she never expected. It was this big, scary, shifting thing.

She strummed her fingers over Wren's pussy lips, enthralled by the silkiness, and focused her mouth on Wren's clit.

"Fuck me," Wren whispered.

Amanda slipped two fingers inside her slowly. The heat was incredible. Wren's pussy contracted around her digits as Amanda stroked Wren's G-spot.

"Am I doing okay?" Amanda asked.

"Yeah." Wren threaded her fingers into Amanda's hair, loosening the messy bun, causing her hair to come free and skim over Wren's thighs. "It shouldn't be so hot that you've never done this before, but it is. You're doing so awesome."

Amanda smiled and suckled Wren's clit, happy that Wren was enjoying it. Wren's legs trembled around Amanda's ears.

"Harder," Wren gasped out.

"Which?" Amanda said, not sure if Wren wanted Amanda to fuck her harder or suck harder.

"Both."

It took Amanda a minute to figure out how to coordinate her mouth and hand in the most effective way, but once she got it, Wren cried out.

Amanda figured this was as good a time as any to use the vibrator. She would have happily serviced Wren for hours, but her jaw was getting tired. She needed to work up some stamina, and she would have done so happily.

Too bad she only had two more days to practice.

With her index and middle finger on her left hand in Wren's pussy and the Fingerslip vibrator on her right index finger, Amanda went to work. Wren's body tensed, her legs jerking straight out, when Amanda ran the vibrator over her clit for the first time.

"Hell yeah, pretty girl. Keep doing that. Gonna make me come."

Amanda didn't want to miss the chance to feel Wren's orgasm on her tongue, so she licked around her fingers lodged deep inside Wren. She circled the vibrator around and around Wren's clit.

Wren's pussy was tight, squeezing her. Then suddenly it fluttered, and all the tension left Wren's body in long, pulsing waves that Amanda rode with eagerness and joy.

Once Wren had stopped twisting and moaning, Amanda removed her fingers but not her mouth. She never wanted to remove her mouth, happy to catch the remnants of Wren's pleasure on her tongue.

Wren rubbed a thumb over Amanda's eyebrow, then down her temple. She sighed, and it sounded like contentment to Amanda's ears.

"You're a nice little slut, aren't you, baby? Cleaning me up," Wren whispered, tenderness in her voice. Amanda liked that way too much. "Come up here and kiss me."

Amanda moved so fast it was as if her body reacted before her brain. She didn't know why Wren's words had hit her the way they did. It didn't feel like they were about sex because they'd both come already, and Amanda was totally satiated. No, Wren's words felt like romance, the kind that was dirty and perfect. The kind Amanda had coveted for so long, and that made the confusing lust in Amanda warp and grow and overwhelm her.

Chapter Seven

Wren watched Amanda get dressed. That was a kind of intimacy Wren had never clocked before. Everything felt intimate with Amanda. Everything felt different. Like it could be more.

That was what Wren wanted. Wren would have to hold onto her hopes, keep them safe. Once this girls' getaway was over, she would remember all these moments, cherish them.

Until then, though, she was going to put her mouth on Amanda's body as many times as Amanda would allow.

"I love those earrings," Wren said. They were blue pompoms. She could tell they were vintage. The rest of Amanda's outfit seemed modern—high-waisted black cigarette pants, a cream sweater, and black heels—but that pop of whimsical retro was so *her*.

Amanda blushed. "Thank you. They're my newest

find. Got them at the antique shop down the street from my apartment. I had to have them."

"What about them appealed to you?" Wren wanted to know everything about Amanda.

"I have a picture of Twiggy hanging in my room. In it, she's wearing one of those quintessential mod mini dresses, and she has the short hair, and the winged eyeliner, and these huge yellow bauble earrings. When I saw these blue ones, they reminded me of that picture."

"They're perfect on you. Very fun."

"You're the fun one," Amanda said, flirtation in her voice.

Fun. Not serious. A vacation fling.

Wren's phone rang, distracting her from her pity party. A picture of Benji cheesing for the camera flashed on the screen.

"Hi, Benji," Wren said as she answered it.

"Wren, my boyfriend ditched me to make money. Please hang out with me."

"What do you want to do?" To Amanda, Wren said, "Benji is bored."

"I don't know," Benji said, a whine in his voice.

"We'll meet you at the lodge in a few minutes. I think they're having a cider tasting and other shit like that today."

"*Boring.*"

"Benji!" Wren said, laughing. He was such a loveable brat.

"Boring, but I'm looking forward to it, I mean. Love you. See you soon." He hung up.

Wren shook her head, unable to stop her smile. Benji would make the afternoon interesting, and it was probably a good idea for them to leave their cottage for a while.

"Are you ready to hang out with Hurricane Benji for a few hours?"

"Sure." Amanda leaned in and kissed Wren. "As long as you're there, I'm there."

If only that were true for longer than New Year's Day.

They made it to the lobby of the lodge a few minutes later to find Benji lounging in the atrium reading a holiday edition of *Midwest Living*.

There was a large easel sign with a schedule of the happenings for the day. Wren read through them quickly. On the far side of the room, registration for an event was in progress. All the attendees were receiving a plastic wine glass with a company logo on the side, and people were drinking from their cups after they entered the event space. It seemed like all you had to do to make it through the door was grab a wine glass and a name tag, which was shoddy security if you asked Wren.

She turned back to the schedule to see the event was called *New Year, New You: Finding Your Light and Self Through Conscious Intentionality.*

So that sounded like a load of bullshit, but she was going to get free wine and a cup out of it.

"Come on," she said to Amanda and Benji. They both thankfully followed her without question. She loved when a plan came together.

She marched up to the name tag table and grabbed three. She passed one each to Benji and Amanda.

"Here you are, Kassi May," she said, reading the tag she gave to Amanda. "And Ben. Ha!" She handed that one to Benji. Her own name tag read *Ashley*.

Then she picked up a plastic wine glass as she breezed in the door. She was happy to see Amanda and Benji followed suit.

"What are we doing?" Benji asked.

Wren turned to find Amanda with a huge smile on her gorgeous face. Wren loved when people got on board with her crackpot ideas.

"Gettin' a free drink. Come on."

Almost everyone else in the room was wearing business casual, so Wren and Benji, in particular, stuck out, but no one stopped them as they got their white wine.

They sat in some chairs in the back of the room while other people milled about. On each chair was a notepad with a numbered list and the words "New Year, New You: Goals and Resolutions" at the top.

"Welcome, welcome, welcome, my family!" a white man said from the stage at the front of the room. He was in a three-piece suit but was barefoot. "Please find a seat and center yourself for the journey ahead."

"Wanna take bets on if this is a cult, a business retreat, or an MLM?" Wren asked.

Amanda snorted into her drink. "What do you think they're selling? This terrible wine?"

"It is bad, isn't it? I like the cup, though." The wine

glass had an ugly logo on it that gave them no hints about the direction of the event.

"As I'm sure you all know, I'm Dr. Astral Smith," the man said.

"Astral?" Benji whispered, and they laughed. "Quick, finish your drinks so I can get us seconds before it gets weird."

To Wren's delight, Amanda downed her drink and handed her cup to Benji.

"Thank you for being brave," Dr. Astral Smith said. "Thank you for understanding that you can reach a higher plane of conscientiousness."

"Did he say *conscientiousness?*" Wren asked. "Maybe this is an etiquette workshop." Wren finished her drink and passed her cup over to Benji.

He stood up and rushed to get a refill.

"Everyone should stay in their seats from this moment forward," Dr. Astral said, a hardness in his artificially floaty voice.

Wren and Amanda both whipped around to see Benji freeze with the three full wine glasses balanced in his hands. He tiptoed back to Wren and Amanda, sending them into a fit of giggles.

"Your rules for the next ten hours include no speaking unless given permission, no leaving your seat unless given permission, and absolutely no cell phones. The purpose of today is to learn to wallow in your discomfiture."

"Yes, nothing says new year, new you like discomfiture," Wren said under her breath, loud enough for Benji and Amanda to hear.

"Let's start by closing our eyes. Imagine the thing you most want to change in your life."

Wren glanced around. Both Amanda and Benji had closed their eyes, but Amanda was still drinking her wine, a smile on her face.

Wren closed her eyes and, surprisingly, complied with Dr. Astral Smith's instructions. She thought about her loft apartment, which she loved. Her career. Her roller derby team. Her friends.

She didn't want to change any of those things, but sharing them with someone would be nice. She would probably have to change some things to finally convince a partner or partners she was worth the trouble, though. No late nights. No drunken tattoos. No sneaking into freaky self-help workshops.

She didn't want to change herself or to tone it down, but she was tired of being lonely.

"Okay. Open your eyes. Let the light of your new understanding underwhelm you," Dr. Astral said.

Underwhelm? Wren had no idea if the word had been intentionally used, but it made Amanda choke on her wine.

"Now, turn to your pads of dreams," Dr. Astral whispered, his lapel mic picking up his voice quite clearly.

What the fuck were pads of dreams? Wren glanced around to find the others in the room messing around with the notepads that had been left on their chairs.

"Write out your resolutions for next year," Dr. Astral continued. "Think about what *you* can do to improve your existential existence. What can you change? Be brave! Be bold! What will most help you earn the life you deserve as children of Mother Earth? What about that evil thing the universe calls 'money?' Do you need it? How can you get more of it?"

Wren peeked over at Benji's pad of dreams. He was making a grocery list. Amanda was leaning over hers, her hair obscuring it from Wren's view.

Wren took a deep breath and started writing. Her first resolutions were ones she always picked and usually fulfilled.

- Grow the business in ethical and inclusive ways.
- Finish a new line of lingerie.

It was the resolutions that followed that hollowed her out. They didn't feel right, in her gut, even as she was writing them.

- Exhibit ability to be serious and commitment-worthy in next relationship.
- Think before I leap into relationships.

The last resolution was the easiest one to write, and, she realized, the one that was most important to her in that moment.

- Fix friendship with Amanda so this getaway doesn't ruin everything.

"Wonderful, wonderful. Thank you for being so brave," Dr. Astral said. "I know how difficult it is for you to be honest with yourself … Now tear up those resolutions. Do it! Rip them to shreds. They. Do. Not. Matter."

Wren was so surprised by his instructions she actually followed them.

"Throw the shreds in the air! Anoint your neighbors with your failures."

The crowd did so, creating a snowstorm of paper around the room.

"What the fuck?" Benji gritted out under his breath, shoving his grocery list in his pocket. Wren laughed and tossed her resolutions at him.

She turned to Amanda to see her frozen there with her paper neatly folded in her hand.

"I don't want to rip them up," Amanda whispered.

"Then don't." Wren laid her hand over Amanda's, closing the paper more firmly in her grasp. "Keep 'em."

"Failures!" Dr. Astral shouted. "Successes! Disappointments! Money! Grief! Contentments! Here at GLOF, we know how to live a better life. It starts and ends with you. It starts and ends with your network of contacts. Your circle of friends and family. It starts and ends with"—Dr. Astral produced a large cannister with a flashy label from inside the podium— "Smart Body Energy Booster Health Powder."

"Oh fuck, it *is* an MLM," Wren groaned.

A man in front of them shushed her over his shoulder.

Wren downed the last of her wine. Amanda and Benji quickly did the same.

"Let's blow this popsicle stand," Wren said.

Amanda nodded, and Benji was already up and out of his chair.

They rushed through the back of the room and practically fell through the door in laughter, Dr. Astral Smith's reprimand echoing behind them.

Once they were out of the banquet hall and safely in the bar, Benji held up his plastic wine glass. "What do you think GLOF stands for anyway?"

"Global Lifestyle Opportunity Fulfillment," Amanda said.

"Really?" Benji said, kind of agog.

"No!" Amanda laughed. "I put a bunch of enlightenment gibberish words together."

Wren giggled and put her head against Amanda's shoulder. Amanda rested her cheek on the top of Wren's head. Benji's eyes went big, and Wren scowled at him.

"I can check 'sneaking into an event I'm not invited to' off my bucket list," Amanda said.

"You need to get out more," Benji said. "That event sucked. We'll find you a fun one next time."

"That was plenty fun for me." Amanda smacked a kiss on the crown of Wren's head. "Just the right amount. Thank you, Wren."

Chapter Eight

When William found Amanda, Wren, and Benji at the bar at six, they were all a few sheets to the wind and avidly waiting for karaoke to start. Amanda had never done karaoke, but she was looking forward to it like a kid waiting for Santa's sleigh.

"What is going on here?" William asked after Benji laid a huge kiss on him.

Amanda sighed. She loved kissing. She wished she could kiss Wren like that.

Wren sat up straight from her slump against the bar. "We were in-doctor-i-na-ted into a pyramid scheme this afternoon." She spoke very slowly like she wanted to get all the words correct.

"Early bird karaoke is about to start, William. Sit down, sit down," Benji said. "Amanda's going first. It's an oldie resolution or something."

"An old year's resolution," Amanda explained.

"Yes. That. Babe, when you take over this bar, you

have to keep early bird karaoke."

Wren and Amanda nodded.

"It's so fun," Wren said.

William glanced around. "It hasn't even started yet, and the bar is empty."

From the stage, a woman in a black polo shirt with the Father Time Farm and Resort logo on it, said, "Howdy folks, welcome to our last karaoke session of the year! We're so excited to have you all here this evening. We're going to start things off with a bang! Up first is Amanda, singing"—the woman glanced at the screen in front of her—"Mariah Carey … Oh goodie."

Amanda skipped to the stage. She realized that the bar was in fact pretty deserted. There were a few elderly ladies, two bartenders, a couple making out by the door, and her friends.

And geez, how cool was that? She had friends. And those friends didn't care about her family's money, or where she'd gotten her clothes, or which VIP restaurant she could get a table at.

And she had Wren.

Beautiful, bubbly Wren.

Wren, whose kiss hit her with the force of a train. Every single time.

The song lyrics appeared on the screen in front of her, and she almost lost her nerve. But no, this was happening.

She sang the breathy beginning of Mariah Carey's "Auld Lang Syne." It was impossible to do Mariah Carey justice, but luckily, no one was paying her much attention besides Wren, Benji, and William. Once the tempo sped up and the instrumentation transitioned into dance music, Wren dragged Benji to the stage.

They stood directly in front of Amanda, arms around each other's waists, and swayed while singing along with her.

Her voice wasn't great. She could match pitch … if it were a normal non-Mariah Carey pitch. So yeah, it wasn't amazing, but it was fun.

By the end of the song, William had joined Wren and Benji, a crowd of three cheering her on and singing with her. She belted the end just for them.

It was something she never would have done before, so that was a check off the old bucket list. If she had one.

The only list she had was the one she'd made in that wackadoodle GLOF workshop this afternoon. A list where she'd spelled out her dreams of opening a vintage clothing store, of quitting her job, of figuring out how to live closer to Wren.

Fairytales, more like, but she was holding them close to her chest.

Once she'd finished her song, Benji was up. He sang "Funky New Year" by the Eagles. William watched Benji like he hung the moon as he strutted and danced over the stage.

Wren was anxiously awaiting her turn. As Benji's song wound down into spoken word, she turned to Amanda. "Wish me luck."

"Good luck." Amanda leaned in and discreetly kissed Wren's cheek.

Wren's face bloomed with the prettiest blush ever.

"What song are you gonna sing?" William asked, snapping them out of their moment. His eyes were lit up with mischief, and Amanda assumed he'd seen the kiss.

"'The Final Countdown.'"

William snorted. "I'm sensing a theme. Isn't it weird to sing New Year's Eve songs on December thirtieth?"

Wren playfully gasped. "Course not. This is the last early bird karaoke of the year, William O'Dare! Get on board."

Benji wrapped up his song, and the MC called Wren to the stage. She shout-sang the whole glam-band rock song, jumping from side to side on the small stage.

Amanda was a smitten kitten. She couldn't stop smiling up at Wren. Couldn't stop cheering.

Toward the end of the song, Amanda caught William staring. She sent him a questioning smile.

He shook his head slowly. "You're good for her."

Amanda blinked. "How so?" She had to shout over Wren's rendition. Then she wondered if that was a stupid question. Maybe she should have asked, "In what way?"

"She's happy when you're around."

"Isn't she normally happy?" Wren seemed like the most happy-go-lucky girl in existence.

"It's different."

Amanda didn't have time to question William about that because Wren's song ended, and they all whistled and cheered for her as she bounced off the stage. Her eyes were bright and her short, dark hair untamed. Her eyeliner had smudged slightly, but it looked intentional and pretty.

Wren put an arm around William's shoulders. He had to lean down for her to reach.

"You're next," Wren shouted in William's ear. One of the old ladies had taken the stage to sing a Tenacious D song.

"Absolutely not," William said.

"Please?" Benji begged, giving William very effective puppy-dog eyes.

"Once you sing, we can go hang out in a nice cozy cottage away from all these pesky people." Wren gestured grandly to the almost empty bar.

William groaned and headed for the bar, where he promptly acquired a shot. After he threw it back, he took his butt over to the binder of songs. Wren followed him.

Within a few minutes, William got his chance to reluctantly trudge on stage. Amanda didn't know what to expect, but when William opened his mouth, she was surprised.

He held the mic earnestly, gazed right at Benji, and started to sing a sweet, plodding ballad.

"What's this song?" Amanda asked. William had the best voice among them. It was simple and sincere.

"It's called 'My Dear Acquaintance,'" Wren said. "I've never heard it, but he was adamant."

Amanda found herself lost in the words of the song. The entreaty to have love, joy, and cheer in the new year, the way the lyrics were directed to "my dear acquaintance," like William was singing just for Benji. Amanda turned to Wren and let the music wash over her. Wren watched her right back.

There were so many things Amanda was reading in Wren's eyes, but that might have been the alcohol. She was probably imagining things.

They were posted up at the end of the bar, Wren's back in the corner and Amanda in front of her. No one seemed to be paying them any mind, everyone too intent on William and his heartbreaker voice.

Amanda wanted to kiss her. She was sure Wren could read it on her face because she took a deep breath and glanced around intently like she was checking for spies.

Amanda geared up to duck in and lay one on her. Wren's mouth tipped up in an ornery grin. Then, quick as a blink, she lifted her shirt and flashed Amanda.

A laugh burst from Amanda's throat. She was so shocked and delighted by the naughtiness of it. Amanda turned to see if anyone had noticed, but they were completely isolated, completely ignored.

"You're bad," Amanda said, a tipsy giggle in her voice.

"You liked it."

"Of course. I like you."

Wren paused, her smile faltering. Or softening. Amanda wasn't certain which. "I like you too."

"Good." Amanda nodded. That settled it.

———————————

Two hours later, Amanda was lying down with her head in Wren's lap in the living room of William and Benji's cottage. They had a skylight. Amanda couldn't see the stars through it, but she enjoyed seeing the reflection of the flames from the fireplace flicker in the glass.

"What about this?" Benji asked. He was modeling his clothing options for the party tomorrow night. He also had his sister, Rosie, on FaceTime.

The outfit he was showing off was black jeans, a purple brocade suit jacket, and a solid black T-shirt.

"Pass," Rosie said from the phone that William was gamely holding up.

Benji frowned. "I like this one."

Amanda thought it looked fab on him. Benji was an odd mix of manly and delicate. He was a big, muscly mechanic, but there was a playfulness in his style.

"You've got something wilder up your sleeve," Wren said. She was running her fingers through Amanda's hair. "We know you do."

Benji grumbled and returned to the bedroom.

Amanda closed her eyes and listened to William, Wren, and Rosie chat. Rosie was evidently a kindergarten teacher with a boyfriend who was an artist. So far, Rosie had sounded forthright and practical. Amanda was excited about meeting her tomorrow.

"Did you and Leo go to Robin's yesterday?" Wren asked Rosie. It took Amanda a second to remember who Robin was. She owned the sex toy company that was the center of Wren's friend group.

"Yeah," Rosie said.

Wren scratched lightly through Amanda's hair. "How was it?"

"Oh, you know, it was an orgy. Always a good time."

Amanda's eyes popped open, and she sat up. "An orgy?"

Silence followed Amanda's words.

Wren and William shared a look, and Rosie sighed. "Talk about making a first impression," Rosie said baldly. "I'm sorry. That was TMI."

"I've never been to an orgy." Amanda turned to Wren. "I should add that to my GLOF New Year's resolution list."

Wren laughed. "I think an orgy is a great resolution. If I thought we could swing it, I'd say it could be your next old year's resolution, but I'm not the orgy queen. I can't magic them out of thin air like some people."

Benji groaned, having evidently just returned to the room, and everyone's eyes whipped to him. "Please tell me we aren't talking about orgies with my big sister. *Again.*"

"That outfit is nice," Rosie said. "Anything else?" She was obviously trying to end the conversation.

"Now wait a minute," Benji said. "You're supposed to help me!"

Amanda liked this outfit better than the last. It was a pair of slim-fit suit pants, a black velvet jacket, and a crisp white shirt. It wasn't quite as showy, but it fit him to perfection.

All of Wren's friends were stupid hot.

"Oh!" Wren rushed to Benji, and they proceeded to whisper with each other, a happy gleam growing in Benji's eyes with each gesture of Wren's hands.

He turned on his heels and disappeared into the bedroom.

"I'm not sure I trust your scheming, Wren," William said, his voice foreboding.

"Oh. *You will.*"

"What did you suggest?" Amanda asked. Wren settled back down next to her.

"You'll see."

Benji rushed back out of the bedroom a few minutes later, and everyone gasped. He was still wearing the same pants, velvet jacket, and white dress shirt, but the shirt was unbuttoned to midabdomen.

Underneath the white shirt was a leather harness crisscrossing his chest. It had fine silver ring connectors.

"Yes!" Wren pumped her fist. "I knew that would be fucking awesome."

"Bravo, Benji. You look great. Wear that," Rosie said from the phone. Amanda nodded.

Benji glanced at everyone, a small slip of vulnerability in his eyes. His gaze landed on William, who was staring at him with a stunned expression.

William slowly stood up. To Rosie, he said, "You don't need to see what's going to happen next. Love you. Bye." He hung up and tossed the phone on the couch, Rosie's laugh abruptly cutting off. He stalked toward Benji.

"You like it?" Benji grinned. William's only response was a sexy grumble. Benji laughed and said, "Oh no. Not in front of the ladies, mister."

William kissed him anyway.

"All right, you two. Save it for tomorrow night," Wren

said. She jumped up and pushed between the men, fussing with Benji's shirt. "Can I take a picture of you and put it on my Instagram?"

Amanda assumed that meant Wren had designed the harness. It was in line with Wren's normal stuff, a mix between soft and hard.

"Wait! Let's do that on New Year's Eve. I'll fix my hair tomorrow," Benji said.

Amanda tried to imagine herself in a leather harness, but she couldn't quite make it compute in her brain. Wren, on the other hand, would appear in control and tough and sexy.

"Okay, sweetheart." William kissed Benji over Wren's head. She gave him a dirty look. "Go change out of this, and we'll order dinner."

Dinner ended up being pizza from a local place a few miles away. It was smart to eat because Amanda needed to sober up if she was going to talk Wren into sex again tonight.

And she undeniably wanted sex.

She had under forty-eight hours to spend with Wren, and she was going to make the most of them.

Though this was pretty nice too. Leaning into each other while they ate greasy supreme pizza and drank soda. The laughter of long-time friends. The sparkle of snow outside the large windows.

"Your turn, Wren," Benji said. "If you could go anywhere in the world next year, where would it be?"

Without missing a beat, Wren said, "Napa."

Amanda's heart tried to launch through her chest in a

spray of confetti.

"Why Napa?" William asked. "You're not that into wine."

"That's where Amanda lives."

"*Ooooh.*" Benji smiled. "Good choice. I'd go to Prince Edward Island."

"Dare I ask why?" William said.

"*Anne of Green Gables.* Duh. Who's turn is it in the hot seat?" Benji let his gaze flit over everyone before landing on Amanda. "Dream job, Amanda. Go!"

"Selling vintage clothes," she said easily. Wren nudged their shoulders together.

"That sounds cool. You should do that," Benji said. "I'm sure being the disco ball princess—"

"Heiress," both Wren and Amanda said at the same time, but Benji soldiered on.

"—is awesome, but I'm a firm believer in finding a job you love. Or at least don't hate. We spend most of our adult lives at work. Your workplace should be somewhere you want to be."

"It's not that easy."

"Why not?" he asked.

"Benji," William said warningly like he didn't want Benji to push too hard.

Amanda patted her pocket where her list of New Year's resolutions was hidden.

There were so many reasons why it wasn't easy. She didn't want to disappoint her parents. She was so used to being the perfect daughter and following the rules. Opening a clothing store—a *secondhand* clothing store, at that—would embarrass her parents to no end. She could just imagine her mother's voice. *No daughter of mine …*

But it was much easier to talk logistics with Benji, William, and Wren than spread her fears at their feet.

"Well, I'd have to rent a storefront, but rent in my area is nuts. I would need to bulk up my stock. My godmother told me I could buy her closets, but that's not enough to fill a store. Plus, capital is—"

"Wait, wait. What do you mean, buy your godmother's closets?" Benji asked. He was smiling at her like she was the most interesting person he'd ever met. She wasn't used to genuine interest in what she had to say. Not from anyone in her real life. It was unnerving.

"My godmother is Myrna Mets. You might have heard of her. She's this eccentric rich lady who's been a friend of the family for ages. Never been married. Owns a bunch of vineyards and is in the society pages all the time for being outrageous. She lives in a big mansion, and every closet is full of her old clothes. She never throws anything away, so she has prom dresses she made for herself in 4H before she was rich *and* vintage Chanel. It's nuts. She's always loved me, and I love her. We bonded over clothes and how annoying my mother is."

"And she's willing to sell you her old clothes to help you get started?" Wren asked.

Amanda grimaced. She realized she'd never told Wren that. It had just felt like a silly dream until this girls' getaway. Now it felt like it was within reach if only she could handwave away her other problems.

"Or be my business partner. She believes in me."

"Myrna's Closet. Name of your store," Wren said. "That's better than Mothball Barn by a mile."

A funny feeling spread through Amanda's chest. She loved that name, and the fact that Wren had suggested it made it even better.

William pointed his piece of pizza at her. "You need a business plan. Lucky for you, I'm amazing at them. I helped Wren with hers when she was starting out."

"Toot, toot," Benji said. "That's William's horn."

"Oh, I couldn't let you do that," Amanda said. This was all moving a little fast. "You hardly know me, William."

"We're friends." He shrugged like it was nothing, but it was sort of everything.

"You could start with an online storefront," Benji said. "You don't have to worry about building rent right off."

"Oh, and you could do pop-up shops," Wren chimed in. "I should get you in touch with Robin and Sasha, Benji's other sister. She's the head of marketing for Lady Robin's Intimate Implements. They do a lot of cool and innovative stuff without having a permanent storefront."

"Whoa, whoa, whoa," Amanda said. Her head was about to spin off. She pressed a palm to her forehead. "This is just my silly dream. You asked about my dream job. It's not actually …"

"Actually what?" Wren asked gently.

"Possible."

Wren's eyes made a circuit of her face. Amanda felt like she'd disappointed her. "Anything is possible."

Amanda fake smiled. "Okay, it's surely someone else's

turn in the hot seat."

Benji blinked a few times, his gaze ricocheting between Wren and Amanda. "Yep. Let me tell you about the sponsorship opportunities I've gotten for my Insta. I'm an *influencer*. Did you know that, Amanda? I influence."

Amanda knew her fair share of influencers. High society kids, who made their money taking pretty pictures and curating their presence for the internet. In an alternate universe, that would have been her route. She could have modeled her vintage clothing finds for her followers, but she was a bit too closed-off for that.

None of the influencers she knew were like Benji.

He regaled them with funny stories about lingerie and followers and Instagram censorship.

Amanda tried not to peek at Wren through it all, but it was hard. Ugly insecurities were bubbling up inside her. Worry about being seen as boring or shallow or spoiled. Or worse—that she *was* those things, not just that people might view her that way.

Hours later, after the pizza and soda were gone, Amanda's awkwardness had finally started to wear away. She and Wren were sitting on the edge of William and Benji's hot tub with only their feet and calves in the water because they didn't want to walk to their cottage to get their swimsuits.

Benji and William had gone inside to put together a cheese tray, leaving Amanda and Wren alone. William and Benji's cottage had a kitchenette, and Benji was very excited about the charcuterie board he'd planned.

"I'm going to run to the bathroom," Amanda said.

Wren was quiet, but it no longer felt uncomfortable. More like she was sleepy and content. She smiled, nodded, and touched Amanda's hand briefly.

As Amanda slipped into the cottage, she heard Benji's voice, needling and filled with excitement. She paused to eavesdrop.

"But, William, that building by Mount would be a great retro clothing store. Can't you imagine? The neighborhood is so neat and quirky, and it would be the right size."

"Amanda lives in California, remember?"

"She could move."

A rushing noise filled Amanda's ears. Her stomach swooped at the realization that they were talking about her, and her face went up in flames.

"She's not going to move, sweetheart."

Amanda pressed herself against the wall and tried to slow her breathing.

Benji growled. "Why not? She *should* move! Have you seen the way Wren looks at her?"

"I know. Typical of Wren to fall for someone so ..." William huffed. "It sucks."

Amanda wanted to shout. "Someone so *what?*" But her breath had left her at the other bomb William had dropped.

The one about Wren falling for her.

Amanda wasn't sure what she was feeling, but maybe, just maybe, it was happiness.

Chapter Nine

Wren gazed up at the stars as she and Amanda walked to their cabin. It was very dark out here, much different than the perpetual light pollution in the city. There was no one around since it was well after midnight. Technically, it was New Year's Eve. The shock of that date spread through Wren. Her time with Amanda was running out.

That was okay. Wren would live. Now she knew what it was like to be with Amanda, and that was worth the pain of their impending separation.

She wouldn't trade the seeds of her crush blooming into full blown flowers for anything. It had been worth it.

Amanda tangled their hands together, and Wren's heart pounded double-time. She had no idea what to say or do, and that wasn't Wren's usual state, chatterbox that she was. Maybe her problem was that she wanted to beg Amanda to stay longer, or to do long distance, or to give her—*this*—a shot.

But Wren's heart was bruised. Too many failed

attempts. She'd been told too many times that she was too wild to tame, too flippant to have a serious relationship.

Amanda pulled her to a stop as they reached a wooden garden arch covered in white twinkle lights.

"Are you mad at me?" Amanda asked. She was wearing one of Benji's large sweatshirts since her coat was still damp and smelled like chlorine.

"Of course not. Why would I be mad?"

"Because I'm a coward when it comes to the clothing store stuff."

"You're not a coward. You're practical. I think that's allowed, babe."

Amanda bit her lip and glanced up. Wren checked out the creamy expanse of her exposed throat. She longed to kiss it.

"Starting with an online storefront is a smart idea. I could sell on a site like Etsy or eBay, but having my own spot, even if it's digital, sounds nice."

"That's an inspired idea. Lots of good things come from the internet."

"Like us."

Wren nodded. She rubbed her thumb over Amanda's knuckles.

Amanda took in a hitching breath and pointed at the arch above them. "Mistletoe."

"What?" Sure enough, they were under a ball of it. "Do you think it holds its power after Christmas?"

"It lasts through December, at the very least," Amanda said primly.

Wren laughed. "Is that why you stopped here?"

"Yeah." Amanda smiled, and it was slightly crooked. "May I?"

"I'd be mad if you didn't."

Amanda kissed her. She held Wren's face between her chilly hands and whispered her lips over Wren's. Their breath mingled, billowing in clouds around their heads. It was a sweet kiss. A kiss that didn't scream sex but made Wren's body tremble all the same. Amanda swept her tongue into Wren's mouth, taking control, using her height and hands to tip Wren's head back.

She tasted like cherry pop and temptation, and Wren would have happily stood in the cold all night if it meant she was the center of Amanda's world. If it meant she would get to experience Amanda's hot mouth, and smell her amber-and-cinnamon scent, and feel her strong hands and soft body.

Amanda pulled back, and Wren chased her mouth, keeping her eyes closed. Amanda didn't leave her hanging, thank God. She rubbed a thumb over Wren's bottom lip and trailed her mouth to Wren's jaw.

"Thank you for this getaway. It's already been my best New Year's Eve, and the day is only an hour old," Amanda whispered into Wren's ear, sending a cascade of shivers down her spine.

"You're welcome."

"You're the most fun. You're amazing." With that, Amanda gave Wren another peck and dragged her toward their cabin.

Fun. There was that word again. Wren liked that Amanda thought she was fun. She wanted to be fun, but she worried it was also an easy reason to write her off. That was the last thing Wren could stand—being dismissed by Amanda Ellis.

It was better to remember that, to hold herself apart. This was a fling, nothing more. A fling Amanda obviously needed.

They tumbled inside their cottage, the adorable Chalet, and Amanda pressed her into the door of the conference room.

"Old year's resolution: I want to fuck on the junior executive table," Amanda said softly, almost shyly.

"Holy shit." Wren laughed. "Okay, I am *so* in. Do you trust me?"

Amanda grinned. "Of course."

"Do you trust me to use a toy on you? They're all sterilized except for the ones we've already used together, which I won't use on you."

"Yeah. I don't have a lot of experience with them."

"That's okay. I'll be gentle." Wren's smile was sharp and anything but gentle. "Go in there and wait for me. Be a good girl and take your clothes off. Leave your underwear."

Amanda shuddered at being called a *good girl*. There was a lot more where that came from.

Wren rushed upstairs and gathered supplies. She was about to return to Amanda when an idea hit her. Wren didn't wear her fancy shit that often, but she'd brought a few extra lingerie options for the New Year's Eve party. It always made an event feel special if she was wearing something cool underneath her clothes.

She wanted tonight to be special too.

Now the question was—should she go naughty or nice?

She changed quickly, catching a glimpse of herself in the mirror. Heat pooled in her belly, and her hair stood on end. She looked hot and fierce and ready to fuck.

Which was perfect. It was exactly the vibe she intended to give off.

When she opened the door to the conference room, a gasp caught in her throat. Amanda was sitting on the edge of the table facing the door, her legs crossed elegantly and hanging off the end. She was wearing a pale pink silk lingerie set. Both the bra and underwear were simple, wearable, and low fuss. It was high dollar, though. Wren could tell with a single glance. The set was very Amanda. The bra had full cups and wide straps to support Amanda's rather substantial breasts, and the panties were cut to reduce panty lines. They showed that she was practical but liked her underthings to be pretty and chic.

The thing that was really blowing Wren's mind, though—Amanda had left her black pumps on.

"You look—"

"Oh my—"

They both stopped talking and stared at each other.

"You're blowing my mind, Wren."

"Why?" Wren set her bag of goodies on the conference table beside Amanda.

"Because your strappy getup … I could only imagine it in my wildest dreams."

"That's me," Wren said. "Wildest." She plopped down in the leather office chair at the head of the table and rolled right up to Amanda's legs.

Amanda spread them because she was an angel fallen from heaven and put her feet, still in those fuck-me heels, up on the arms of the chair.

Wren was helpless but to kiss her ankle, to worship the transition between foot and shin and knee with her lips. She trailed her mouth up the inside of Amanda's thigh.

This setup was making Wren feel bossy. Well, bossier. She had a tendency to be overbearing in bed, but right now she felt like the CEO about to ravish her darling secretary.

As Wren pressed her face to the juncture between Amanda's thighs, there was a tickle on the back of her neck. Amanda was tracing the satiny bamboo straps of Wren's bralette, focusing on the halter that encircled her throat.

They were polar opposites—Amanda in a prim and sensible silk set, Wren in a super strappy blood-red one with an honest-to-God collar. Wren liked that about them. She liked that they were different but fit so well.

She just wanted them to fit outside of bed too. To match. To stick.

But she couldn't think about that. She'd promised Amanda a getaway, a fling to literally fling away the expectations and pressure exerted on her. She'd promised Amanda a rocking New Year's Eve, and she planned to deliver.

Without a word, she pressed her mouth to Amanda's

pussy over her panties, letting her breath ghost over the silk. Amanda had to slam her hands down behind her on the table to catch herself.

"You gonna soak these pretty little panties for me, Amanda?" Wren asked before latching on to Amanda's clit and sucking.

"Oh God" was all Amanda seemed to be able to manage.

Wren nuzzled her. "I love how wet you get when you come. The way you taste. You deserve someone to live under your desk at the office, to work you over every day like this."

"Yes. Wren, fuck."

Wren glanced up to see Amanda staring at her avidly. "Do you trust me?"

Amanda nodded.

"If you don't like something I do, or if you're unsure, all you gotta do is say so. I'll stop right away."

"Okay."

Wren reached into her bag and pulled out a sliver of silk. It was the belt to a dressing gown, but it would do the trick.

She held up the tie. "Can I put this around your eyes?"

"Yes." Amanda's chest was heaving, her breasts straining the cups of her bra. Wren wanted to peel that bra off with her teeth.

They got the tie situated and comfortable.

"You can pull it right off if you need to," Wren said.

"I know."

"Good. Lie back, but keep your feet planted on the arms of the chair."

Amanda followed directions, sending a pulse of power through Wren's chest.

She hooked her fingers under the crotch panel of Amanda's panties and speared them into her. Amanda's pussy was soft and slick with arousal, and it clenched around Wren's fingers.

"You like my fingers in your cunt?" Wren asked, stroking gently over Amanda's G-spot. Wren was dirty talking, but she also wanted to know. Some people could take it or leave it. For Wren, she would normally forgo fingers for something bigger and blunter, but it would also be nice to be finger-fucked every once in a while. Sweet, almost.

"Yes … I can come this way." Amanda said. She squirmed.

"Can you now? You're just a needy slut, huh?" Wren whispered, trying it out to see how Amanda took it.

Amanda's mouth dropped open, and she panted, a pink blush glazing her cheeks. She was sin incarnate with her eyes covered and her sex face on. Jesus Christ.

"I love that you're needy, baby. I love the way you're writhing on my fingers. You're perfect."

Amanda's hands scrabbled over the wooden surface of the table trying to find purchase, and her pussy started that telltale fluttering, so Wren pulled her fingers out. Amanda really could go off like a party popper, which delighted Wren to no end. The fact that Amanda had complained about her partners in the past not making her come made Wren wonder if they'd even fucking tried.

"Oh geez," Amanda breathed, rolling her head against the table.

Wren reached up and dabbed a bit of Amanda's own arousal on her parted lips. Amanda licked at it desperately.

"What are you feeling, pretty girl?" Wren asked, selecting a toy she hoped would blow Amanda's mind.

What was Amanda feeling? She had no idea.

Nothing.

Everything.

Not being able to see made Amanda very aware of her own body, of its needs. Its demands. Every sensation was staggering, including her own taste on her lips.

"I don't … I can't talk," she managed to gasp out.

"That's okay. As long as you feel good."

"I do."

A sudden buzzing reached Amanda's ears. She assumed it was a vibrator, and her assumption was verified as Wren pressed the toy lightly against her leg as if to warn her.

"Tell me if it's too much," Wren said.

Amanda nodded. Wren moved the crotch of Amanda's panties to the side again and pressed a few fingers back inside. It felt so damn satisfying and way more intense than normal. That had to be the blindfold, but maybe it was also Wren. The shape and strength of Wren's fingers, the fact that Wren definitely knew her way around a pussy.

Amanda squeezed her inner muscles around the digits, wishing they were thicker, that she was full to bursting, but also recognizing that this felt too awesome to wish for anything else.

Wren traced the tip of the vibrator up the inside of Amanda's groin. It felt smooth, small, and cylindrical. *A bullet*, Amanda's brain provided helpfully like she'd suddenly acquired a bunch of sex toy knowledge. Amanda tried to arch toward it, but Wren tutted, and Amanda fell back onto the table, breathless.

Wren finally rested the tip of the vibrator against Amanda's clit. Her panties muted the sensation slightly, which was a good thing because it almost made her jump out of her skin.

She had used a vibrator before, of course. Once she and Wren had gotten to know each other well enough to share secrets, Wren's enthusiasm for them had made Amanda curious. But masturbation was usually just a perfunctory means to an end, and a vibrator simply made the process efficient. She'd never used one with a partner, which was probably a red flag for those past relationships and the way she'd kept herself and her desires locked away.

"That's it, Amanda. The way you move is so sexy, showing me what you need."

That was the key, wasn't it? Wren was reading her

body, listening to it. Wren made her feel like she was important, like her desire was.

Wren circled the vibrator around Amanda's clit. Amanda realized she was rotating her hips, chasing and retreating from the sensation and forcing Wren to move her fingers in and out.

Hunger caught her like a fishhook, tugging at her sharply. "More," she managed to grit out. "Want to be full."

Wren set the vibrator down—it rattled against the fancy conference table—and used her free hand to pull Amanda's panties farther to the side.

"Want to watch you take my fingers," Wren said. Her voice was wrecked. Heat flushed down Amanda's spine.

Wren pulled out and thrust back in gently. Amanda had no idea how many fingers Wren was using. Maybe three? But it wasn't enough. Wren fucked her roughly a few times.

The sound of Wren spitting knocked against Amanda's senses before she felt the saliva hit her pussy. That was not something Amanda would have ever thought she would like. Hell, she'd never thought about it before, but it was so dirty, and it dinged this deep, wanton place in her brain, lighting her up.

She arched and had to grab onto her own hair, to grab onto anything. Another finger nudged her pussy, pushing at her. An image of her opening up like a blossom flashed behind her eyelids. Wren let go of her panties, fingers still planted, and picked the vibrator up from the table.

That extra finger, not quite inside her yet, but trying, *teasing*, nearly pushed her over the edge. The vibrator on her clit did the job.

A shudder tore through her, and her body locked hard around Wren's fingers before releasing in a flood of endorphins and tremors and moans.

Wren didn't remove the vibrator, which seemed to make Amanda's body jerk and pulse forever.

"That's right. Take it, pretty girl. Doesn't that feel good?"

Eventually, with a whimper, Amanda twisted away from the toy, and Wren let her go, slipping her fingers out at the same time.

Wren gently kissed the inside of Amanda's thigh. "Reach down here and feel the mess you made of your panties, love."

Amanda obeyed without thought, her mind snagging on Wren's use of "love" as a pet name. The silk was wet and slippery. "Fuck."

"You know how hot that is? How hot you make me? I think I could come, and all I've done is finger you."

Amanda smiled and slid the silk blindfold off her eyes. "You did a bit more than finger me." She had to blink several times to allow her eyes to adjust to the lights in the room. This room didn't have the mellow lighting of the rest of the cottage. It was slightly harsh, which made her realize that she'd been completely on display. And that turned her on more.

She was learning all kinds of things about herself, and that was down to Wren. Wren had made this safe for

Amanda. Safe for her to let go, to be herself. To feel pleasure without her insecurities and fears making chaos in her head.

Somewhere in Amanda's head, a ball was dropping, ready to light the sky with fireworks. This safety … this openness was how relationships were meant to be. It was how *this relationship* could be.

Amanda lifted up on her elbows and stared down at Wren where she was sitting in the leather office chair. She was shocked again by the sight of Wren in her strappy, red bra and matching G-string. She wasn't even sure if you could call that thing a bra. It didn't have cups but a horizontal mesh band over the center of Wren's breasts and vertical straps that crossed over her chest and neck.

Wren grinned and crawled up onto the table, straddling Amanda's waist and kissing her. Amanda took this for the gift that it was and touched as much of Wren as she could. The knobs down her spine, her hipbones, her pierced nipples covered in mesh, her butt.

The kissing, though, was life-changing. Maybe it was the floaty feelings from an incredible orgasm, but Amanda let her mind spin away from her, let herself imagine a life where she had a vintage clothing store across from William's famous gay bar.

A life where she spent every night in Wren's bed. Where she got to kiss this amazing woman's lips every day. A life full of friendship and comfort and great sex.

Wren made a noise in the back of her throat and pressed her pussy against Amanda's stomach.

"What do you need?" Amanda whispered against Wren's lips.

Wren ripped her mouth away and tried to catch her breath. Her eyes were glassy as she glanced around the room.

"Go grab those decorative books for me," Wren said, pointing at a bookshelf on the far side of the room.

Amanda hopped to it, but the books weren't books at all. "It's a box." She held up the container, fashioned to look like the spine of old books.

"Even better." Wren reached into her bag and dragged out a large green dildo.

"Is that Shrek's?"

Wren laughed. "Yeah. I love this baby. It's got a wicked head."

Amanda handed over the box, and Wren plopped the green dildo onto it, testing its suction cup. Wren seemed to be happy with it because she pushed the box-and-dildo combo to the end of the table and rifled through her bag.

Amanda took the time to analyze the dildo. It was thick and bumpy with prominent veins and a pronounced head. It was also a beautiful, swirling green color.

"You like it?" Wren asked as she knee-walked over to the box and dildo. She had the Fingerslip vibrator from that morning and a bottle of lube. She handed the vibrator over to Amanda and doused the dildo in lube.

"Yeah," Amanda breathed. She would love to sit on that thing, but she was more enthralled with watching Wren prepare it for herself.

Wren pulled off her panties and straddled the dildo,

her knees near the edge of the table. Amanda stood directly in front of her. Wren's eyes fluttered closed as she slowly sank down on the monster dick.

"Kiss me," Wren gasped.

Amanda knew Wren meant she wanted a kiss on the lips, but Amanda's mouth was watering for something different.

She crouched down so she could get her mouth on Wren's clit, giving it a juicy suck that made Wren freeze her ride on the green dick and groan.

Wren twitched her hips slightly. The angle wasn't great, and Amanda could taste lube, and yet, she loved this. Wren grabbed Amanda's head and held her steady.

"Suck harder," Wren said. Amanda obeyed. If she flicked her tongue out far enough, she caught the side of the dildo, and an image of Wren riding a random person's dick while Amanda went down on her flitted through her brain.

It was a daydream, not something she even knew she would enjoy, but it was so hot and perfect, that image. It was joyous, this taking and receiving of pleasure in all its forms. That was what Amanda craved, and she wanted it with Wren by her side.

"I want you," Amanda said because she *had* to. "I want this."

Wren moaned and pulled Amanda up until they could crash their mouths together, their teeth clanging and a tinge of blood hitting Amanda's taste buds.

She took Wren's hips in her hands and helped her move on the dildo.

"Yes. Fuck, Amanda." Wren pressed her mouth against Amanda's throat. "Wish we had a strap-on. I could ride you."

"Next time," Amanda whispered.

Wren lifted her head, and they gazed at each other. Emotion passed through Wren's eyes, and Amanda realized she'd never seen Wren look so vulnerable. So open.

"Next time?" Wren panted. "Will there be a next—"

"*Yes.*"

Wren's face twisted, like she was in pain, but Amanda knew she wasn't. Then Wren's hands went wild over Amanda's body. She ripped the cups of Amanda's bra down, pushing her breasts up over the brim, and she dipped her hand back to Amanda's pussy under her panties, as if it was a necessity to feel the wet warmth down there. To play over the slick folds and sensitive skin.

"Please, Amanda," Wren pleaded. "The vibrator, please."

Amanda turned on the Fingerslip and rubbed it lightly over Wren's clit. Wren slammed down on the dildo, the muscles of her thighs pumping. Her small breasts were bouncing as much as the strappy bra would allow, and Amanda needed those babies in her mouth. She caught one of Wren's pierced nipples between her lips.

"Oh yes. Just like that." Wren tensed so hard her body trembled.

Amanda focused on moving her finger with the vibrator on it in circles around Wren's clit. She released Wren's nipple and moved to the other one. With her free hand, she reached down where Wren was stretched around the dildo, caressing her arousal-swollen pussy lips.

Wren cried out and lifted both her hands to Amanda's face. Amanda could smell sex on Wren's fingers, but that thought flew from Amanda's mind because Wren kissed her. Then Wren came, her mouth greedy and her body trembly, burying her cries on Amanda's lips and tongue.

Chapter Ten

Wren couldn't stop kissing Amanda. They'd slept wrapped up in each other and hadn't gotten out of bed for anything besides bathroom breaks, even though it was almost noon. Lazy morning make-out sessions were Wren's favorite, but these kisses reeked of desperation. At least on her part. It was their last full day together. Tomorrow at this time, Amanda would be at the airport.

Wren was so scared of what she'd say if they stopped kissing. She was so scared she'd beg for more and complicate things to no end.

That was the last thing she wanted to be for Amanda —another complication. Not when Amanda was running from all the complications and expectations in her life already. Not when Wren had promised her a fun, stress-free party for New Year's Eve.

Amanda lightly bit Wren's lip and pulled back with a sigh. Her face was scrubbed clean of makeup and her hair was in a messy braid. She seemed fresh and newly formed. Wren felt like she was getting to see a side of Amanda that was secret and *hers*.

"Do you think it's possible to accidentally sleepwalk through life?" Amanda whispered.

Wren rubbed her thumb over Amanda's bottom lip. "Sleepwalking is accidental by nature. I don't know anyone who goes to bed and thinks, 'Man, can't wait to dump food out of the fridge and pee in my closet tonight.'"

Amanda giggled. "Is that what happens when people sleepwalk?"

"Probably. It's your metaphor, hon. What are you really asking?"

"I don't want to be unhappy in my job forever. I'm not sure how I got so stuck. It's just that working for Ellis International Products was what was expected of me. My life selling bulk glassware was carved out before I was old enough to have an opinion."

"Well, new year, new you, Amanda. It's always possible to change course."

"Yeah, I guess."

Wren tucked a strand of golden hair behind Amanda's ear. "It's okay to find other ways to have a fulfilling life. Work that job you maybe don't love, but after work, *outside of work*, have hobbies and relationships and friends who fill that hole in your heart."

Amanda nodded. "I want it all, though."

That shouldn't have made Wren's heart beat the way it did. "You deserve it all," she said, trying to instill passion and certainty into her.

"It's scary to think about a big change."

"You're braver than you give yourself credit for."

"You think so?"

Wren cupped Amanda's cheek. "I know so."

Amanda's phone trilled with an incoming text, and they both jumped.

"I'm normally attached to my phone, but I keep forgetting about it," Amanda said. "Having too much fun with you."

"Same. I'm obsessed with my phone because you're on the other side of it. Now you're right in front of me."

That had been too honest by half and sounded ridiculously romantic. It was true, though.

Amanda's eyes flared. "And you're right in front of me."

They stared at each other for a few long seconds before Amanda lunged at her, rolling her under. As Amanda kissed down Wren's body, Wren had the foolhardy thought that this felt like more than sex.

Of course it felt like more than sex ... *for her*. It *was* more than sex for her.

It was making love, what with the long stares and the needy kisses and the joy. Last night, even with the bossiness and the ogre dildo and the conference table, there had been a tenderness to the whole deal.

Wren couldn't remember the last time she'd made love. Couldn't remember the last time it had felt like love and not simply infatuation or pent up energy or horniness.

But as Amanda took her apart so sweetly and innocently with her mouth and hands and a bit of battery power, Wren knew that at the very least she was falling for Amanda. *Had* fallen for Amanda. And it was scary as fuck.

Two hours later, after a quick rinse in the shower and cleanup in the conference room that they'd skipped the night before, Wren found Amanda standing out in the snow behind their cottage.

She was wearing several layers of clothes, her arms wrapped around her chest, and gazing up at the sky. Wren put on her boots and coat and trudged out there. It was snowing lightly. One of those perfect, storybook snowfalls, the flakes fat and fluffy.

"What are you doing?" Wren asked.

"I haven't seen snow in years. Not since a trip to Zermatt six years ago."

"Where's Zermatt?"

Amanda shrugged, looking bashful. "Switzerland. I went on a ski trip with my parents."

"Oh. Wow." Wren bet that was a fancy-ass trip. "I didn't know you skied."

"I don't. I suck at it, and I get altitude sickness. It was a pretty miserable five days in one of the nicest hotels in the world, to be honest."

"Lucky you get to experience Father Time Farm and Resort then. I'm sure they're comparable."

"This place is more my style," Amanda said. "It's charming. I like charming."

"Me too." Wren stepped closer to Amanda, sharing

body warmth. "So you've got snow. What are you gonna do with it?"

"Anything?" Amanda grinned.

"Old year's resolution, baby."

Amanda ran. "Snowball fight," she shouted over her shoulder.

Wren laughed and followed. The snow was blisteringly cold in her ungloved hands, and it was too powdery to pack, resulting in them throwing handfuls of glittering snowballs that came apart in the air before impact.

They ran around the open area behind their cottage, dusting each other with snow, for ten minutes before Amanda wrapped her arms around Wren's waist and brought her to the ground in a fit of laughter.

Amanda stared down at her. "You have snowflakes in your eyelashes."

Wren blinked, a little breathless. A little speechless. Amanda's nose was pink and cute, her cheeks even rosier. "I don't want this getaway to end."

"Me either," Amanda answered easily, and maybe it was easy for her. It was aspirational. Like saying "good" after someone asks, "how are you?" It might not have been true, but it was nice to hear.

"Have you ever made a snow angel?" Wren asked because it was easier to ask a silly question than a hard one.

"No. Not that I can remember."

"Here. I'll teach you." Wren pushed Amanda onto her back in the snow and straddled her waist. Frigid wetness seeped into the knees of Wren's pants, but she didn't mind. "Spread your arms and legs."

Amanda gave her a cheeky smile and obeyed. "This is a pretty unconventional teaching method."

"It's an old year's resolution. Straddle Amanda Ellis every chance I get. Now move your arms and legs up and down."

Amanda grinned and lifted her appendages out of the snow, then back in the snow, then out again, very purposefully misinterpreting Wren's directions.

Wren laughed and pinned Amanda's arms to the ground and directed their movement, creating wings. Amanda moved her legs herself.

"See?" Wren kissed Amanda's mouth gently. "You're an angel."

"A corrupted one."

"Fallen."

"Very." Amanda kissed her harder.

Wren pulled back. "Have you enjoyed your corruption this New Year's?"

As Amanda considered the question, Wren waited on pins and needles. She needed to hear Amanda say that she'd loved it. That she wouldn't trade it. Wren would hold on to those words, pull them out to admire and remember like party favors once Amanda was gone and their main connection was through cell phone screens and Twitter DMs.

"It's been cathartic. I'm so glad you convinced me to come."

"I'm so glad you said 'fuck it' and hopped on a plane."

"Hello?" a voice hollered from the front of their cottage.

Both Amanda and Wren glanced up in alarm. They couldn't see the yeller, but his voice had carried.

"Who is that?" Amanda asked.

"That, pretty girl, is Leo Whittaker. Let's go. It must be later than I realized."

"You go ahead. I'm going to call my parents real quick. They've been blowing up my phone."

Wren helped Amanda stand up. Both of them had wet spots on their clothes. "You going to stay out here?"

Amanda nodded and looked around. "I like the snow."

"It's cold. I'll get you another layer."

Leo and Rosie came around the side of the cottage, stepping gingerly through the snow. Quick introductions were made, and they all headed toward the enclosed back porch.

Wren retrieved a soft flannel blanket for Amanda, who sat on the back porch steps. Wren wrapped it around Amanda's shoulders, giving extra care to cover the bare spot on the back of her neck.

When Wren turned around and headed back inside, she found Leo and Rosie waiting for her, matching expressions of surprise on their features, their eyes big. She rolled her own eyes and led them into the living room.

Who cared if she was an open book? Amanda went home tomorrow anyway.

———

This phone call with her parents was not going well. They were both on the phone, but her dad was only contributing by saying, "Oh, Amanda," every so often in his disappointed voice.

"I don't understand where this is coming from. Ridiculous," her mom said. "I expected you to be here tonight."

"I told you I wouldn't be," Amanda said. "More than once."

"Guess this dress I got you is wasted money."

"Mom. We've already had this conversation. I didn't ask you to buy me a dress."

A very sophisticated huff sounded through the phone. Her mother, again. "And what is this about selling *used* clothing?"

Amanda had to laugh at the inflection in her mom's voice. "I've got a line on stock to get me started, and I already have a closet full of vintage patterns. I'll start small, but hopefully I can do it full time."

"Oh, Amanda."

She rolled her eyes and smiled. Her parents' usual suspicion and foot-dragging wasn't bringing her down.

"I'm trying to be brave and honest. I don't want to sell wine glasses in bulk to Hollywood event organizers for the rest of my life."

"Ellis International Products has given you a lot, young lady. You shouldn't knock it," her mom said.

"I'm not knocking it. I just want something different."

Her father sighed again and actually said a full sentence with verbs and everything. "What was this remote work idea?"

Amanda pumped her fist. "Okay. Here's what I was thinking."

An hour later, Amanda, Wren, and Rosie were pruning up in the hot tub together, and Amanda was riding high from her conversation with her parents. Leo had disappeared to hang out with Benji and William.

Wren and Rosie had a camaraderie that made Amanda jealous and excited all at once. She'd not had in-person female friends since school, and even then, she'd felt isolated. It was fun to see Wren and Rosie interact. They so obviously loved and respected each other.

At the moment, they were showing off their bruises from their last roller derby throwdown. It was hard to imagine Rosie, who seemed a tad starchy, being a vicious and aggressive roller derby queen.

"I brought you jam," Rosie said suddenly. "It's New Year's themed. I have some for you too, Amanda."

That touched Amanda more than she cared to admit.

"What kind is it?" Wren asked.

"Fig, pomegranate, and grape."

"Wow, that's a lot of stuff."

Rosie smiled. "In Ancient Greece, they smashed pomegranates on New Year's Day for good fortune. And eating twelve grapes at midnight on New Year's Eve is a

Spanish tradition that's supposed to lead to prosperity. And lastly, figs symbolize fertility."

"I was with you until the fertility," Wren said dryly.

"It was what I could find at the grocery store. Not very artisan of me, I know."

"It'll be delicious. Your experiments always are." Wren blew Rosie a kiss, and they both laughed.

The conversation moved to a gallery opening for Leo. It seemed as if Leo traveled quite a bit and that Rosie had met him for the opening in Pittsburgh since it fell over her winter break at school.

"What kind of art does Leo do?" Amanda asked.

There was an awkward extended silence that ended in Wren giggling. Rosie squared her shoulders. "The erotic kind. He's really talented."

"Oh." Amanda glanced at Wren, who was laughing harder, seemingly at Amanda's surprise. "I'm sure he is."

"I'm in his newest collection," Wren bragged. "He painted my hands grabbing our friend Dean's dick." Wren turned to Rosie. "It's gorgeous, isn't it?"

"It's a good-looking dick. And beautiful hands," Rosie said wryly. She laughed. "It's my favorite in that collection. I remember when you two posed for him. He came home, and we—"

"Ahem, ladies." They all jumped at Leo's voice. He had snuck up on them. Amanda had been way too enthralled hearing about Wren's hands and some man's penis to notice his approach. "I hate to interrupt this intellectual conversation about my ... art."

Amanda laughed. Wren's friend group blew her mind a little. She wanted a piece of this.

"What's up?" Rosie said.

"The resort had a cancellation, so we were able to get a room after all. We won't have to bunk with William and Benji."

Rosie smiled at him, something sharp in her eyes. "That's wonderful news. We won't have to be quiet."

Leo blushed, which was very intriguing. "Yep. It's in the lodge and has its own balcony overlooking the atrium, which is cool. It'll be loud from the party, but it's better than nothing. All that to say that you can get ready in our new room or here, if you want. There are options."

"I'll get ready here." Rosie smiled at Amanda and Wren. "It's nice to have a second and third opinion."

Leo gave Rosie a kiss and left.

"We should hop to it, huh?" Rosie said.

From there, it was a whirlwind of dresses and heels and hairspray, interspersed with enough champagne and pop music to make Amanda feel giddy.

Rosie was wearing a maroon tea-length dress with a brocade pattern and a peter pan collar. She looked like a hot and fancy kindergarten teacher, which was pretty much exactly what she was. The thing she evidently needed extra opinions on was her lipstick color.

While Amanda was fixing her hair, trying to give it big, loose curls, Wren got dressed, so it was a surprise when Wren waltzed into the large, elegant bathroom wearing the hottest outfit Amanda had ever seen.

The black mini body-con skirt hugged her narrow

hips and showed off her strong, roller derby legs. She had on black stockings, garters, and ultra-tall chunky heels. The highlight, though, was the completely sheer, loose crop top showing off a black delicate lace bra underneath.

"Wow." That was all Amanda could manage. "Just wow."

Wren grinned and took a slinky step her way, pinning her against the sink. In her tall heels, Wren was Amanda's height.

"I don't want to mess up your makeup," Wren whispered, her lips barely ghosting over Amanda's.

"It's supposed to be kiss-proof."

Wren took that for the permission it was, kissing Amanda sweetly. Amanda couldn't keep her hands off Wren, slipping them inside the crop top and fingering along the lace cups of Wren's bra.

"Oh!" Rosie was standing in the doorway to the bathroom, which had been left wide open.

"Oops." Wren took a subtle step back, and Amanda's hands fell off her body.

"Ha! Leo owes me ten bucks."

Amanda's face flamed, and she could feel the stickiness of her lipstick smeared on the edges of her mouth. What a marketing lie!

"How did you know?" Wren asked her. Wren had pulled on a rakish smile that seemed like a mask to Amanda.

"A hot fling with your hot friend from California. I mean …" Rosie smiled.

"That's very me," Wren said.

"Yeah."

They both laughed, but she could tell Wren's was brittle

"Thanks for calling me hot," Amanda said, trying to change the subject.

"Well, I've got eyes," Rosie said matter-of-factly.

Amanda went about fixing her kiss-messy makeup, and Wren and Rosie left the bathroom to snack on food they'd ordered from room service. When Amanda returned to the sitting area, the mood felt more normal, and her face was no longer hot as an oven.

"I brought two dresses," she said. "I'm not sure which to wear."

"Fashion show, fashion show!" Wren chanted, waving a shrimp with cocktail sauce on its end.

"Okay. Honest opinions only," Amanda said.

"Deal."

Amanda jogged upstairs and quickly removed the hotel robe she'd been wearing. The first dress was a green silk wrap dress. It was from this decade, unlike her other one, and accentuated her curves. She skipped back downstairs to show it off.

"That's beautiful," Rosie said. "Really accentuates your figure."

"Thank you."

Wren smiled. "I like it. Now show us the other!"

Amanda changed into the next dress. If she were being honest with herself, this was the one she was excited about wearing. She'd gotten it from Myrna's closet full of clothes from the 1980s. It was a sparkly silver sheath dress covered in fringe and wasn't as flattering as the other, but she couldn't imagine another event where it would be appropriate. She slipped her glittery pumps on and made her way downstairs.

When she made her appearance, she was met with crickets. "So, no?" she asked finally, standing awkwardly in front of them.

Rosie glanced at Wren, but Wren didn't respond except to smile enigmatically at Amanda.

"They're both pretty on you, but I like the green one better. I'm also boring, so I'm maybe not the best judge," Rosie said hesitantly.

"You were at an orgy two days ago. I wouldn't call you boring," Amanda said, prompting Rosie to laugh. Amanda brushed her fingers along the front of the dress, making the fringe shimmer. She loved this one.

"You have to wear that one," Wren said. She was full-on grinning and staring straight at Amanda. "It's so *you*."

"You think so?"

"I know so."

Chapter Eleven

The New Year's Eve party was busier than Amanda had expected. The core dancefloor was in the banquet hall where they'd had their little MLM protein powder run-in, but the party filtered into the main atrium, where there were high bar tables, appetizer stations, and a cash bar. Partygoers packed into both spaces, laughing and talking loudly over the dance music.

When they arrived and got their tickets stamped, they were each given one drink ticket and a gift baggie full of weird goodies. Now they were posted up at one of the tall tables emptying the bags.

Benji pulled out what appeared to be a tiny champagne bottle. "Oh, look. Bubbles." He popped the cap off and blew into the bubble wand. Bubbles floated around their heads. There were also party hats, headbands with disco ball antennas, novelty sunglasses, and an array of noisemakers.

Wren donned her sunglasses and plopped one of the

headbands on Amanda's head, being very careful of her hair. "There's my disco ball heiress. I love party favors," Wren said, her hand still lightly resting on Amanda's jaw.

It was an innocuous thing to say, but it felt like more, what with the eye contact and the soft touch.

"Me too," Amanda managed to stammer. She glanced down at her bounty. "Breath mints. That's a smart favor with all the kissing at midnight."

Other people around the atrium had also dug into their gift bags, so noisemakers echoed through the room, almost drowned out by the music, and bubbles sparkled in the party lights.

"So … shots?" Benji said. Rosie seemed scandalized by that, but everyone else cheered.

"Shots, shots, shots," Wren sang.

William and Leo dutifully retrieved the shots from the bar, and everyone slammed them back. Amanda was instantly glad she'd eaten before the party, but she needed to stay on top of her alcohol intake if she wanted to have sex with Wren again tonight.

And she definitely did.

Wren might have been thinking the same thing because she waved off a second shot.

"Who are you going to kiss at midnight, Rosie?" Wren asked, a twinkle in her eye.

"Well Leo, of course," she answered primly. "And maybe whoever else we're with."

"Ew." Benji covered his ears and chanted, "La la la la."

Rosie bumped him with her hip. "Sorry you aren't as

exciting as me." Her voice was incredibly deadpan. "Only kisses from William for you."

"I would kiss someone else," he insisted. "If William were there."

William coughed a laugh.

Benji scowled at his boyfriend. "What? I would. We played Spin the Bottle that one time on Valentine's Day, and I kissed a bunch of your friends that night."

"That's true. Whatever was I thinking?" William said.

"I'll kiss someone else right this instant, mister."

William, unperturbed, nuzzled Benji's hair. "We should. Let's all do it. Kiss a person who is not our date. That sounds like great fun." It was clear that William was mostly kidding, but Amanda also suspected that Benji kissing someone else in an agreed-upon manner truly didn't bother William that much.

She felt as if she'd fallen into another dimension, but she liked it. She liked the looseness and comfort these people had with each other and with their partners.

"I'm in," Leo drawled. Rosie nodded, a smile playing over her lips.

"What the hell. Me too," Wren said. Then she glanced at Amanda. "As long as it's fine with—"

Amanda grinned, her smile so wide it hurt. "I'm in too. I can't imagine who I'd kiss, but—"

"God, what a bunch of heathens we are!" Benji laughed. He stomped over to Amanda. "Disco princess?" He tapped one of the disco balls on her headband, sending it springing around.

She laughed. "Uh-huh?"

"May I?"

"Why not?" She shrugged. Benji gently caught her cheeks in his large, callused hands and gave her a simple but sweet kiss on the lips.

She felt bubbly with laughter.

"Thanks." He grinned at her, then turned to William. "Ha! Bet you didn't expect me to kiss a girl. Women have the softest lips."

"I did not expect that. You're right." William snatched Benji to his side and rumbled something in his ear that made Benji turn red.

Wren turned to Rosie. "Lay one on me, Prim Reaper, so Amanda and I can go dance."

Rosie hid her smile by kissing Wren. It lingered a bit more than Benji's kiss had but mostly looked like a greeting among friends.

It sent a zip of jealousy through Amanda. The type of jealousy that revved her up. She enjoyed watching the kiss, which was a shocking twist.

Once Rosie had pulled back, Wren grabbed Amanda's hand and tugged her toward the dancefloor. "Let's go. I don't want to stick around to see the Holiday siblings' boyfriends make out. That's too weird, even for me," Wren teased.

Their friends booed Wren for ruining their fun, and as Wren hauled Amanda off, she glanced over her shoulder to see William, Benji, Leo, and Rosie cracking up and playfully needling each other.

"Your friends are weird," Amanda said. Wren was shaking her hips to the beat as they snaked through the crowd. Amanda longed to palm those hips. To pin them down.

"Sorry about the kissing stuff. I hope you didn't feel pressured or weird about it," Wren said warily over her shoulder.

"No, it was fun. I like them. They're wild like you, but I like you the most."

Wren spun around and threw her arms over Amanda's shoulders. They'd reached the center of the dancefloor. "Do you now?"

"Yes. By a wide margin. I like you a lot."

"Good." Wren's voice went low and possessive. Then her mouth was on Amanda's mouth, and they were more kissing than dancing, but Amanda didn't care. She sucked at dancing, but she did not suck at devouring Wren Rebello.

There was glitter everywhere. Glitter and bubbles and flashing lights. It was everything Wren loved in a party, made even better by the glow in Amanda's eyes and her wide smile. Amanda hadn't stopped grinning from the moment Leo had handed her a shot. Or maybe it was from the moment Wren had stuck that silly headband on her head and said, "I love party favors."

Wren snuck her hand over Amanda's hip, squeezing and kneading the flesh there. Amanda pressed into the touch.

"Only a few hours left," Wren whispered in her ear.

Or close to her ear. Amanda was so tall in those sparkly fuck-me heels that Wren couldn't quite reach it. "Do you want to get in a few old year's resolutions?"

They were posted up on the wall of the event hall, the crowd flowing around them. Amanda pulled Wren in front of her body, Wren's back to her cushy, curvy front, and kissed Wren's neck lightly.

"I think it's your turn," Amanda said.

Wren sighed and closed her eyes, trying to think of something else she wanted to accomplish.

She couldn't. She was too content. Too happy.

"I'm drawing a blank. I'd be happy to stand here with you for the rest of the night."

Amanda drew her arm around Wren's waist. It made Wren feel cherished, which was unusual. She normally didn't let others take care of her, preferring to be in control, to protect herself before her partner realized she wasn't worth the long-term trouble. But she didn't know how to protect herself against Amanda anymore. She needed to. Their time was running out, a literal count-down, but it was so hard to pull away.

She couldn't do it.

"All I wanted was a crazy New Year's Eve like the ones on TV. With champagne flowing, sweaty dance-floors, and ill-advised kissing." Amanda nipped at Wren's neck. "I think I've already achieved that, and it's not even midnight."

"Ill-advised kissing?" Wren said, her heart shooting to her throat. That shouldn't have hurt, but it did.

Amanda spun her around. "Not you." She frowned.

"I literally kissed your best friend's boyfriend two hours ago."

"Oh." She'd forgotten about that. "You're my best friend too."

Amanda laughed, her perfect teeth gleaming in the muted light. "Well, if you had a boyfriend, maybe I'd kiss him as well. But only if you were there and watching me."

Wren bit her lip on a smile. "You liked me watching you? Or being watched?"

"Maybe both?" Amanda leaned in to whisper in Wren's ear. "I've learned a lot about myself on this trip. Thank you for ..." She shook her head.

Wren wrapped a tendril of Amanda's hair around her finger. "For what?"

Amanda leaned back against the wall and regarded her seriously. "I've never trusted a partner the way I trust you. It has ... I don't know ... let me be open to new experiences. To discover that I'm maybe not quite the boring, shallow heiress everyone thinks I am."

"I never thought you were boring or shallow. I've been obsessed with you since you sent me that retro pattern. You're amazing."

A flicker of emotion passed through Amanda's gaze, or maybe it was the changing colors of the party light.

"I trust you," Amanda repeated. "I believe you when you say you think I'm amazing. Do you know how different that is for me? To believe that the person I'm sleeping with values me. *Sees* me. It's ... I don't know how to—" Amanda shook her head. "At first I thought this was so freeing because it's a fling, and I'm on vacation, and I was able to separate what was going on between us from the rest of my life."

"It was an escape. *I was*." Wren yearned to be more than that to Amanda, and maybe that was where this conversation was leading. But she didn't want to get her hopes up. "What do you think now?"

Amanda opened her mouth, but a large presence at Wren's back made her snap it shut.

Wren whipped around to see that idiot who'd been hitting on Amanda in the bar a few days ago. What was his name? Hayden something? William hated him, and he hadn't endeared himself to Amanda either.

He was sweaty and red-faced. His gaze trailed over Wren's body, up and down. Then he dismissed her, his gaze latching onto Amanda like she was a prize he deserved to win.

"You made it after all," he said.

Wren planted her body in front of Amanda. She didn't have any right to, but she wasn't going to let some alpha asshole come at her date. Or, well, her friend. She felt especially murderous considering the conversation he'd interrupted.

"I said I had a ticket," Amanda said.

"I would have given you a VIP ticket," he said. He glanced at Amanda's headband. She hadn't taken it off, and every move she made sent the glitterball antennas dancing. "You would have gotten substantially better party favors and *three* drink tickets."

Amanda laughed. "Is that all?" Her voice was scathing. "I'm good, thanks."

He gritted his teeth. "You'd have had substantially better company as well." He sneered at Wren.

Wren was nothing but amused by this guy's bluster and far, far from intimidated.

Amanda wasn't amused. She was so *not* amused, she feinted at the guy. Wren was so surprised by the sudden movement that she caught Amanda around the waist, expecting her to make contact, and Hayden stumbled back, spilling his drink over the front of his fancy suit.

"You bitch!"

"What?" Amanda asked, suddenly calm as a kitten. "I didn't even touch you."

He stared at her, his eyes wide and confused like he was second-guessing his own memory. Wren laughed again. Amanda's little disco balls were still quivering, but she appeared so placid.

Hayden frowned, spun on his heels, and stomped off.

"What was that, Rambo?" Wren asked once they were alone.

Amanda looked at her shyly. "I didn't like him smirking at you."

Wren pressed her body against Amanda's, pinning her to the wall. "That was nuts, and I loved it way more than I should have. For once, I wasn't the impulsive one."

Amanda put the back of her hand to her forehead playfully. "Oh my, what's come over me?"

"I'm a bad influence."

"You're the best influence." Amanda kissed her

soundly, her smooth thigh sliding between Wren's legs, sliding against her stockings.

Wren's mind spun from the lust, the heavy dance beat, and the desire to give Amanda anything and everything she'd ever wanted. To make this night unforgettable. Their earlier conversation niggled the back of her mind as Amanda cupped the back of her neck and really kissed her.

Amanda had mentioned getting hot at the idea of being watched. Maybe some pseudo-exhibitionism was in order. A plan started to form in Wren's mind. All she would need to do was have a chat with her favorite freaky friends, Leo and Rosie.

Amanda pulled back with a gasp. Her lipstick was flawless, though her lips were wet from their kiss. A rosy blush had spread down her neck, and her eyes were bright.

"I have to stop kissing you," Amanda said. "It'll ruin midnight. I want it to feel special."

Wren couldn't hold back a dirty, irrepressible grin. She slid her fingertips down Amanda's side, slipping over the shimmering fringe of her dress. She let her hand come to a stop on the inside of Amanda's hipbone.

"I'll make it special. I can't promise my mouth will be on your mouth at midnight." She dipped her hand to Amanda's inner thigh, inside the short dress, her thumb rubbing a suggestive circle on the soft skin there. "But I do promise I'll be kissing you."

Chapter Twelve

Amanda spent the ten o'clock hour on fire. She danced with Wren. She danced with Benji. She even danced with Daisy the bartender on one side and Rosie on the other. Then she and Wren spent twenty minutes using up their bubble party favors and making up backstories for different couples scattered around the dancefloor.

She'd never had so much fun. Her voice was sore from laughing and her legs weak from jumping to the beat. It was exactly what she'd wanted in a New Year's Eve, and she couldn't help but think that it was exactly what she wanted all the time.

With Wren, every day would be exciting. Sitting on the couch with Wren was exciting. Talking about their feelings was exciting. There was a lightness in her chest. A *rightness*.

At the beginning of this journey, she'd been able to let go because she'd convinced herself that what she did over New Year's *didn't count*. She was able to shed the facade of perfect daughter, of uptight heiress, because this thing with Wren was a fling with a deadline. She'd allowed herself to open up, to be unafraid because, yes, she trusted Wren as a friend, but also because there had been a haze of unreality over the whole deal.

Well, the haze had lifted, and in the clarity, she saw only Wren.

Wren, who was currently whispering conspiratorially with Rosie and Leo while Amanda admired the sharpness of her shoulders and the messiness of her dark short hair from a distance.

Eventually, Leo handed Wren what appeared to be a credit card, and Wren waltzed back over to Amanda.

"I've got a surprise for you, but it involves leaving the party. Sort of," Wren said.

"Sort of?" Amanda draped her arms over Wren's shoulders. She felt touch-starved, like she needed her hands on Wren all the time or the night would spin out of her control.

"Yeah. We've got a little less than an hour before midnight. Let me show you the surprise, and if you don't like it, we'll come straight back to the dancefloor."

"Is the surprise sexy?" Amanda asked. She'd been thinking about Wren's teasing earlier, about Wren saying she'd kiss her somewhere not on the lips at midnight.

"I hope you think so." Wren winked, which made Amanda reevaluate her opinion on winkers because it was damn sexy when Wren did it.

Amanda yanked Wren forward and planted a quick kiss on her. She couldn't help herself. "Lead the way."

Wren tugged her off the dancefloor and to coat check, where Wren had left a large black purse. Then they took an elevator to the third floor and stopped in front of a hotel room door.

"This is Rosie and Leo's room. I asked if we could enjoy their balcony overlooking the party for a while. They won't be up here for another few hours."

Wren used a keycard to get into the room, which was fancy but lacked the personality of their Chalet. There were three bottles of champagne and several glasses on the entertainment center. Wren snagged two flutes, a bottle, and, confusingly, a fluffy white towel as they made their way to the balcony.

On the balcony, they could clearly hear the bumping of the party. Amanda leaned on the railing and studied the partygoers down in the atrium. The balcony was fairly deep and private. They couldn't see onto anyone else's balcony from theirs, and she suspected no one would be able to see them if they were far enough away from the railing.

"What do you think?" Wren asked as she popped the champagne bottle and poured them some bubbly.

"It's awesome." Her skin was buzzing with anticipation. She wasn't sure exactly what was going to happen up here, but she had hopes.

While Amanda sipped her champagne, Wren rearranged the furniture on the balcony, pushing an armchair and a large adjustable chaise lounge to the back wall and firmly out of view. It was basically fancy outdoor furniture with wooden arms and legs and big blue cushions.

"Come sit with me," Wren said.

Amanda skirted the wooden side table and plopped down on the chaise beside Wren. They drank more champagne, letting the noisy party below reach them.

On an impulse, Amanda dipped a finger in her champagne and painted it over Wren's lips. Wren had been wearing a deep plum lipstick at the beginning of the night, but it had worn off from kissing and drinking, leaving behind a subtle purple tint. Now, those juicy lips parted on a gasp. She didn't lick the champagne off. She just stared at Amanda with heat in her eyes.

Amanda leaned in and kissed Wren very softly, the crisp taste of champagne bursting on her tongue. When she pulled back, Wren's eyes were even darker, the lids heavy.

"I like that game," Wren said, her voice low. She wetted her finger with champagne from her own glass and daubed it along Amanda's collarbone, quickly following with her mouth.

Yearning twisted in Amanda's stomach—a slow, careful thing, like a rope coiled around a hand. Wren repeated the process over the cusp of Amanda's shoulder, down to her wrist, the join of her forefinger and thumb, sucking and licking up the cool liquid and spinning Amanda into a deeper web of hazy arousal.

Abruptly, Wren sat up and reached for her black purse.

"Whatcha you got in there?" Amanda asked. Her voice was thick.

Wren winked. "Party favors."

"What kind of party favors?"

With a grin and lots of dramatic flourish, Wren pulled a … fringed noisemaker out of her purse. It was shiny, cheap, and made of gold foil. She kneeled between Amanda's legs and kissed her hard before pulling back and fluttering the noisemaker over her thigh. She followed that tickle with her lips, nosing the hem of Amanda's dress farther up her leg.

"No one can see us here," Wren said against her leg. "I double-checked."

"Okay." Amanda's breath was coming fast.

"But we can hear them. They could hear us if we really wanted them to. Is that fine with you?"

"Yes."

"And it's all right if I make you come out here on this balcony, party raging below us?"

Amanda thunked her head back on the cushion of the chaise lounge. She felt the disco balls on her headband quiver. "Yes."

Wren flipped up the bottom of Amanda's dress, revealing her underwear. "Oh, lookie here. This is gorgeous." She trailed a finger over the rose-gold silk waistband. "But it's coming off."

Amanda obediently lifted her hips so Wren could strip off the panties.

"God, you've got the prettiest cunt. Has anyone ever told you that? Makes my mouth water, Amanda."

Amanda loved when Wren's voice got gruff and hard. She wriggled a little, torn between spreading her legs wider to show off and the innate shyness that made her want to snap her thighs together.

She took a deep breath and spread them.

Wren gently rubbed a thumb over Amanda's clit, and Amanda melted into the chaise with a sigh.

"Love the way you look right now, half-dressed with that silly headband on," Wren whispered.

Amanda laughed. She felt so happy, so ecstatic to be here, like this, with Wren, she could hardly stand it. "Thank you." She hoped Wren knew she was thanking her for more than the compliment, but maybe she didn't. As Wren bent down and kissed over Amanda's clit, Amanda gasped. "For everything. For this whole girls' getaway ... Oh fuck. For making me feel happy and free. Damn ... And for being you. *Yes. God, Wren.*"

Wren chuckled and slipped a finger into Amanda's pussy. "You're tight," she said, her breath hot against all of Amanda's most sensitive skin.

"Oh?" Probably because she was wound up.

Wren laughed again and pulled her mouth away slightly. "I want to get as many fingers in you as I can. Been dreaming of it. Want to stuff you so full of me you feel me on that plane tomorrow."

Amanda moaned. "*That.* Yes."

"But I think you need a nice orgasm to relax first, huh? Bet I could make it quick. Get you off, real pleasant-like, then do it all over again but better. You want that, pretty girl?" Wren finished that fantastic monologue with a nipping bite to Amanda's inner thigh.

"Okay," Amanda managed to gasp.

"Just okay?"

"Better than okay."

Wren settled more comfortably between Amanda's thighs and latched onto her clit with a hard suck. It was so shocking that Amanda cried out, but Wren didn't let up.

She went at Amanda with a quick and efficient vengeance. With relish.

And like all the other times Wren had done this, Amanda found herself immediately on edge. Her thighs trembled around Wren's head, and Amanda held her breath. She was gripping the sides of the chaise so hard her knuckles ached.

Relief burned through her like a cleansing fire. She let out a mix between a yell and a sob, and all that tension snapped in quick, short bursts. Her clit pulsed on Wren's tongue, and the din of the party turned to static, only flooding back once her heartbeat slowed.

Wren sat up, grinned, and gently thrust her index finger back into Amanda's pussy. Amanda twitched weakly, but it felt amazing. "Yeah, see? Nice and relaxed and ready for me. Did that feel good?"

"Yes. So good." Amanda's fingers and toes were still tingling. She glanced down at her toes and realized she'd lost a sparkly pump during the tumult.

"That's what I like to hear." Wren stood up next to the chaise and shimmied her skirt up to reveal sexy garters attached to the bottom of lacy boy shorts. She unsnapped the garters from the underwear with no fanfare, leaving them swinging from the tops of her black stockings. Then she pulled her panties off and playfully tossed them at Amanda.

Amanda caught them, which was surprising. Her reflexes felt molasses slow. "For me?" she said, fluttering her eyelashes.

Wren laughed. "Only the best for you." She took two steps over to her black bag and dug around.

"What else you got in there? More party favors?"

"You bet." Wren pulled out a fancy little box. It really did seem like it could be a party favor.

Or jewelry.

Wren popped the box open and retrieved a delicate metal charm.

"What is that?" Amanda asked.

Wren held it up for her to see. It was a pair of tiny tongs with black silicone on the ends and a fanciful heart at the join. "It's a clit clamp."

"Oh!" Amanda looked down at herself, bewildered and uneasy.

"No, it's for me," Wren said in a rush. She laughed and blushed. "I didn't realize I had this one with me until I dug through my stash last night. It, umm, well—it increases my sensitivity." She fiddled with the clamp. "Makes everything intense and amps me up. It also makes it easier for me to come without vibration, but I haven't gotten much chance to use one with someone else. I thought it would be fun to wear it while I keep playing with you."

"Yeah," Amanda breathed. Now that she knew it wasn't for her, she was fascinated. "I want to see you put it on."

The blush on Wren's cheeks deepened. "Not sure it's that sexy of a show, but okie dokie." She kneeled in front of Amanda, facing her, and spread her knees far apart. Then she placed the silicone pinchers around her clit and slid a metal ring toward the tips to tighten it. It seemed so simple, and Wren was so matter-of-fact, but as she let go of the clamp, she sucked in a hissing, unsteady breath. Her eyes darkened, her expression sultry as she met Amanda's gaze.

"What does it feel like?" Amanda whispered.

Wren smiled crookedly and retrieved a bottle of lube from the bag. Then she maneuvered the white towel she'd grabbed under Amanda's butt.

"You know that moment right before you come, where your clit is throbbing and at its most sensitive?"

Amanda nodded. "Yes. You've been quite adept at soliciting that sensation from me the last few days."

"Ha! Well, *that*, but without coming. It's a bit of a mindfuck actually, but I like it." Wren peeked at her phone and smiled.

"What's on the phone?"

"Just checking the time. Don't worry. It's not midnight yet." Wren kissed Amanda, delving into her mouth in rhythmic thrusts. It was rougher than their previous kisses, like Wren couldn't hold herself back. Amanda relaxed farther into the cushions and accepted whatever she could get.

Wren slid her mouth to Amanda's ear. "I'm going to finger fuck you now. That okay?"

"Yes." Amanda shivered at the gravel in Wren's voice.

"If it hurts, you need to tell me immediately. If you want more, tell me that too. Yes?"

"Yes."

Wren sat back. The smile that bloomed over her face was as vivid and blinding as the party lights. "I'm going to make you feel so good, baby."

She drizzled lube over her fingers and tenderly entered Amanda. It felt like two fingers, maybe. Not enough to stretch. Wren had been right—having an orgasm earlier had made her body lax and malleable.

It was pretty simple, bare-boned bliss. Fingertips stroking over her G-spot, a thumb that occasionally ghosted over her clit. Amanda closed her eyes and enjoyed it.

After a few minutes, Wren added more lube and another finger. It stretched her slightly, but she quickly adjusted. The increased pressure inside made the muscles in her stomach jump. She was wet and messy from the lube and her own arousal.

"You like that?" Wren asked, speeding up her thrusts slightly.

"Yeah." Amanda trailed her hands over her own body, feeling the fringe on her dress swing and slip between her fingers. She touched her own breasts. Their weight in her palms was nice, and she especially enjoyed Wren's shaky gasp at the sight.

Amanda opened her eyes. Wren was flushed, and her

mouth was swollen from the kisses and from biting her lips. Wren's skirt had dropped back into place, obscuring her gorgeous pussy and the little clamp from Amanda's eyes.

A sneaky sort of anticipation started to unwind inside her. She could come from internal stimulation alone. She knew that from lots of practice, but usually it took just that—*practice*. Yet, she felt like her body was reaching for something, aching for it.

"Wren … more? Please?"

"You want my pinkie, needy girl?"

"Yes. But slow."

Wren kissed Amanda's upturned knee. "Of course." She drizzled extra lube over Amanda's pussy without pulling her fingers out, making a mess over her hand and the towel below. It made everything deliciously dirty.

With subtle nudging, patience, and all her focus on Amanda, Wren got another finger inside her. Amanda could tell Wren's fingers were scrunched close together, and the stretch was unbelievable.

A moan cracked through Amanda's chest as Wren worked the fingers deeper. More lube. More gentle thrusting.

"Oh my God." Amanda couldn't hold her head up any longer, even though she'd quite enjoyed watching Wren in action. Her body felt weak and vulnerable.

She really liked it.

"Are you okay, Amanda?"

"*Uhnf.*" Amanda had to blink a few times. That

unwinding pleasure inside her had nearly reached the end of its rope, beginning to pull taut. "Good. I'm good."

Wren let Amanda adjust. Let her body start to sing with wanting more. With wanting deeper.

"Feels like your whole hand is up there," she said thickly.

"Just about. Everything but my thumb. Think you can come this way? You're doing amazing, baby. So perfect."

"Yeah. I could … but I want the thumb."

Wren froze for a second, and under other circumstances, Amanda might have gotten self-conscious, but she was too far gone for insecurity.

"You sure?"

"Uh-huh. Please."

"Have you ever done that before?" Wren asked.

Amanda shook her head. Her hair stuck to her sweat-kissed skin.

"I'll go slow, and I'll stop if it doesn't feel good. I promise."

"Trust you," Amanda guttered out.

Wren slowly pulled her fingers out and doused her entire hand with lube before quickly getting back to where they'd been before. Amanda's body accepted her fingers again easily.

She felt the bump of Wren's thumb against her entrance. It was pressed tight against Wren's palm.

"Deep breath, beautiful," Wren said. She sounded so in control, and that was what Amanda needed. She needed to let go. She needed to fly.

Suddenly, she was stretched so wide it hurt, but it was

also indescribable. Like Wren was reaching a hidden depth inside her, touching her somewhere that no one else could. Like Amanda was made for Wren's fist.

The stretch eased as quickly as it appeared, then nothing but pulsing relief. They both gasped. Amanda managed to open her eyes, her vision hazy. Wren was looking avidly down at her pussy.

Amanda must have made a noise because Wren glanced up.

"You … Fuck, Amanda. Can't describe how hot it is to see you around my wrist."

Amanda couldn't say anything. Her ability to speak was gone. She was shaking, her insides tensing and releasing. The fullness was incredible, but she craved movement. She twitched her hips, drawing another gasp from both their mouths.

Wren added lube around her wrist and slowly, almost imperceptibly, moved her arm.

The pleasure wasn't like anything Amanda had ever known. It was deeper, more internal, and it was peeling out on her fast, ready to speed away. She was afraid of it because it felt big and terrifying.

"Close," she choked out. "Scared."

Wren hummed. "Don't be scared. I'll catch you. I'm right here, pretty girl."

A cheer from the crowd below went up, and Amanda jumped. She'd forgotten they were down there. Forgotten where the fuck she was. That there was an entire New Year's Eve party not three floors below her.

They were counting down. "Ten … Nine."

The adrenaline of it all tightened her body, and she moaned, long and low.

"That's it. Come for me, A. Almost midnight."

Wren caught one of Amanda's hands with her free one. Amanda hadn't realized she was flailing until Wren's fingers curled around hers.

"Six … Five."

Amanda stared at Wren. She was shaking so hard, and Wren's hand felt so fantastic. It was too much.

"Four."

Amanda cried out. She came before the crowd below said "three." Long, hard pulsing waves crashed over her. She was completely unwound, a wire snapping from the pressure, releasing her from its hold.

A massive cry went up from the crowd below, yells of "Happy New Year."

Balloons and confetti fell from the ceiling in a kaleidoscope of color, passing the opening of their balcony.

Amanda was making loud, shocked noises, pleasure ripping through her slower now, but no less strong, and Wren reverently kissed her palm, her eyes closed, like Amanda was the most precious thing in the world.

Chapter Thirteen

Wren's wrist and forearm were soaked in Amanda's release, which was about the sexiest thing in the whole fucking world. Second only to the noise Amanda had made as she'd popped. Or maybe her O-face. Or maybe it was the trust implicit in what they'd done, the trust Amanda had given to Wren. Actually, it was all good. It was all amazing, and Wren wasn't capable of quantifying it.

She removed her hand and fingers slowly, taking her time, but Amanda hardly made a sound. She looked blissed out and wrecked.

Wren used the towel to wipe them both off. It was lucky she'd thought to put it down because they'd been messy.

She snuggled up to Amanda and held her as she came down from her high. Wren's clit clamp was creating insistent and hard-to-ignore sensations, but she pushed it to the back of her mind, riding out the unresolved yearning instead. Cuddling Amanda was just as fulfilling.

Amanda was still wearing that ridiculous headband with the disco balls, but it was noticeably off-kilter. The sight was so sweet and perfect that Wren felt her heart dislodge like a champagne cork and go flying around the balcony.

Wren carefully took the headband off and kissed Amanda's temple. Amanda sighed and nestled closer. They laid there a few minutes before Amanda stirred, her eyes groggy.

"Let me get you some water, love," Wren whispered.

Amanda frowned and shook her head. "In a second." She trailed her palm down over Wren's breast, sending a zing of pleasure to the pit of her stomach. Amanda's hand kept going, finally reaching Wren's thigh, where she halfheartedly tried to push her skirt up.

"It's okay, Amanda. We don't have to do anything else."

Amanda grumbled, and her frown went adorably deeper. "I want to. Wanna go down on you while you're wearing that clippy thing."

"A clamp."

"That," Amanda said. "But my body is all loosey goosey." She snapped her fingers, and Wren laughed. Wren loved Amanda like this—fucked out. "Sit on my face."

"Excuse me?" Wren said playfully.

"Yep. Make this lounger thing recline all the way back

and sit right here." Amanda made a popping noise with her lips.

Wren cranked the handle to make the lounge lie flat. She still wasn't sure about this, but her body was screaming at her to saddle up.

The silly sleepiness had cleared from Amanda's eyes. "I'm serious. I would love to make you feel good, Wren. I want you to be on top of me, and in my mouth, and everywhere."

That was convincing enough. Wren yanked her skirt up around her waist and gingerly straddled Amanda's neck and shoulders.

"Anything I need to know about this sucker?" Amanda asked.

"My clit?" Wren said, a tease in her voice.

Amanda laughed. "The clamp!"

"Not really. You'll probably make me come just by going down on me, but if you remove it when I come, my orgasm will be stronger."

"And all I have to do is slide that ring down, and it'll come off?"

"Yep." Wren brushed her fingers through Amanda's hair.

Amanda smiled. It was such a tender smile that Wren didn't expect Amanda to grab her ass and pull her forward to her mouth.

"Oh fuck!"

The prickly, pulsing sensation in her clit multiplied tenfold with Amanda's lips on it. She rolled her hips, and

Amanda moaned her approval and clutched at Wren's ass.

Every brush of Amanda's lips, every suck and lick, was a lightning rod to her core. She realized she was making these gasping mewls, but she couldn't stop.

She cupped the back of Amanda's head and rode her lips hard. "This okay?" she asked, her voice shot.

"*Mmhmm.*"

She was getting close. It was mind-blowing, and she was getting close.

Amanda must have been able to tell because she tried to get her fingers up the clamp, but with Wren's arms holding her head, there were too many appendages in the way.

Wren let go of Amanda and planted her hands a foot above Amanda's head, so she was on all fours.

Amanda brushed against the clamp with her fingers, and the tug on Wren's clit sent her eyes rolling back. So close. So close.

Amanda murmured, "Tell me when."

And Wren gasped out, "When. Now. When."

Amanda got the clamp loose, and Wren's nerve endings exploded. She trembled through her orgasm, grinding against Amanda's sensuous, sucking lips. She felt like a popped balloon. A noisemaker at its loudest setting.

A soothing caress on her thighs brought her back to reality, and she slipped to the side so she didn't smother Amanda with her pussy.

"That was so hot," Amanda said, staring up at the ceiling above them. "You screamed."

Wren laughed. "I did?"

"Yeah. And the party is quieter now that it's past midnight. People might have heard you." Amanda said this like she was delighted by it.

Wren was kind of delighted by it too.

She kissed Amanda, tasting herself on Amanda's lips. "Happy New Year."

"*Mmmm.*" Amanda slipped Wren a little tongue before pulling back with a smile. "Happy New Year."

"Want to go back to the party?"

Amanda laughed and rolled her head on the cushion underneath her. "I want to get in bed with you. Does that make me a spoilsport? Not exactly life-of-the-party material here, I guess."

Amanda might not have been the life of the party, but that moniker had been following Wren for her whole life. Tonight, though, she didn't want to be anywhere except under the covers with Amanda.

"You just had my whole hand inside you. I think a bed is warranted."

"That was unreal, by the way. I would love to do it again. Maybe next time we see each other."

Wren tried not to jump at that. She'd been working under the assumption that this was a fling. Maybe Amanda thought they could be the type of friends that fucked every time they met up. Wren wasn't brave enough to imagine Amanda wanted more than that, but even the inkling of possibility was causing a conga line in her chest.

"Let's go to bed," she said, rather than, "Yes! Girlfriends forever!" which was very measured on her part, she thought.

They did a quick cleanup and righted Leo and Rosie's balcony. As they left the hotel room, Wren shot Rosie a text that they were done.

She got back the winking emoji with its tongue out, which was very unlike Rosie but also apt. Then Rosie responded, *Take your time. We've found other ways to entertain ourselves. Might not make it back to the room, regardless.*

Wren shook her head and smiled. She loved her friends.

She and Amanda made it back to their cabin before one o'clock. An early night for Wren, at least when a party was involved, but she was excited to dive into bed.

They both went about their bedtime routines in companionable silence, including a quick, shared shower. Wren put on an old pair of mesh athletic shorts and a long-sleeved T-shirt. Amanda put on a different silky sleep set, this one with wide-leg gauchos and an oversized menswear-style top with ribbing and buttons.

Neither were dressed to incite lustful thoughts, but Wren thought Amanda looked like a bedtime goddess. It made her imagine all kinds of retro-inspired silky wonders she could create for the woman in her bed.

That was a dangerous thought, though. One she'd have to stress over in private tomorrow.

Once the lights were out and a small fire banked in the fancy fireplace, they lay facing each other in the big, cozy bed.

Wren was exhausted, and Amanda seemed exhausted

too, but neither one of them closed their eyes. Wren didn't want to go to sleep. In less than twelve hours, this would be over in one way or another. She planned to milk every moment of consciousness.

She reached across the middle distance between them and tucked a strand of wet hair behind Amanda's ear, lingering for as long as she could get away with.

"I'm so glad you came, Amanda. Thank you. This has been a dream come true."

"For me too." Amanda's eyelids were heavy, but she was obviously fighting sleep. "This one bed situation was the greatest, happiest accident."

Wren smiled. "It was."

Amanda blinked slowly a few times. "I don't want us to end tomorrow. I want you to be in my life."

"I will be. You're my online bestie, Amanda Ellis."

Amanda shook her head. "I mean more than besties."

"Oh." Wren's heart started to race. "What?"

"I told my parents I want to work remotely. We could be together. I'd move." Amanda yawned and snuggled closer, closing her eyes. "Then I could open Myrna's Closet, and wham, bam, thank you, ma'am. New Year's resolutions—achievement unlocked."

"Oh."

"That all you're gonna say?" Amanda struggled to open her eyes, but she managed it. There was humor in her expression. Humor and trust.

It was the trust that got to Wren. Amanda trusted her, and Wren wasn't going to betray that trust by allowing her to do something rash.

"Hey." Wren rubbed Amanda's cheekbone with her thumb. "That sounds like … wow. Really awesome. And God knows I've had a full-blown crush on you for five years. But—"

"You have?"

"Uh … Yeah. Sorry. Hope that's okay."

Amanda's smile indicated it was.

Wren swallowed the need to kiss that smile and powered on. "But I'm the queen of reckless decisions. Of not thinking things through. Not thinking about consequences. I've gotten burned so many times because of that. I couldn't live with myself if you made a life-changing decision because we had fun over New Year's."

Amanda seemed alert now and more than a little annoyed. "So what? You want this to be over? Just a hookup?"

"No!" Wren scrubbed a hand over her face. She was not explaining this well. "Not at all. But I think you should take a step back. Take a breath. Not make any hasty changes because of a bit of good sex."

"It was more than sex for me." Amanda's voice had gone stilted, like after she'd fallen in the pool.

"For me too. And fuck, I hope we can continue to be more than that. I do, Amanda. But still. I've always been written off for being out of control and wild. We had an intense night. It's been an intense few days. I don't want to let the *fun, fun, fun* part of me dictate this. You need to think about this, to be sure that I'm … that *this* is what you want."

The fire in the fireplace flickered, sending a wash of

light over Amanda's face. There was a watchfulness there as if she was puzzling something out.

"It has been an intense night," Amanda said. "I'm sorry for forcing a define-the-relationship convo on you."

"No." Wren cradled Amanda's face in her hands. "Don't apologize. I want you to be honest." She kissed her softly. "I ... I care about you so much. Let's get some sleep."

Amanda kissed her back, but it felt bittersweet.

Chapter Fourteen

Morning came fast and hard. Amanda's whole body ached but in a nice way. A way she would latch onto once she was on the airplane and flying away.

Last night's conversation had not gone according to plan, and they were acting wooden and unnatural with each other as they packed their bags. Something that Wren had said last night kept scratching at Amanda's brain, but she couldn't quite grasp it to form a full thought.

After about the third "excuse me" as Wren skirted Amanda to get to her toiletries in the bathroom, Amanda had had enough.

She dragged Wren into the sitting room and pulled her down onto the loveseat.

"We're okay, aren't we?" Amanda asked.

"Of course."

"Kiss me." It was demanding, but Amanda didn't care. If Wren was evidently okay putting this on hold so they could cool down after an intense few days, or whatever her reasoning was, Amanda wanted to get in as many kisses as possible.

That crooked smile Amanda loved so much tripped over Wren's face. She kissed Amanda on the nose. Then the chin. Then finally the lips.

"I would like to go with you to the airport, but I can't figure out how to juggle your rental car," Wren said. "Maybe I could Uber back here after we drop your car off?"

"That's a lot of effort."

Wren's eyes went dim. "Yeah."

Amanda wished she could smack her hand over her mouth and stuff the words back in. "If you don't mind doing that, I would love to say goodbye at the airport too."

"Yeah?" Wren repeated, this time with hope in her voice.

"Yes. I've always wanted a big romantic aeronautic goodbye."

"Well, then by God, I'll give you one." Wren smiled and kissed her again.

That, at least, seemed to break the ice. They spent the rest of the morning trading kisses and lingering touches. Wren disappeared for a few minutes to chat with William about something that was evidently pressing. When she returned, her eyes were slightly red, but her smile was easy and open, so Amanda ignored it.

She was ignoring lots of things. As they drove to the

airport, she started to add them up in her head like a list of resolutions.

- Wren's red eyes
- Wren's insecurity last night
- All the talk of being wild and fun as if it were a bad thing

That bothersome hitch in her brain still felt just out of reach by the time they returned the rental car. Wren walked with Amanda along a covered causeway from the rental car place to the airport proper. They held hands.

Once Amanda got her ticket and there was nothing to do but say goodbye, tears pricked the back of her eyes, heat spreading down her face. She was a hot cryer. Her whole face would turn ruby, and she would feel like she had a fever. It wasn't pretty, and it was about to happen.

Wren didn't seem to be in better shape. Her perfect, pointy chin was trembling.

"We'll talk as soon as you land," Wren said.

"About us?" Amanda asked.

Wren's lips tightened. "Sure."

That wasn't exactly an enthusiastic agreement, and Amanda had the disorienting realization that she might need to cut her losses here. It was clear that Wren didn't trust Amanda to know her own heart, and she wasn't sure what to do or what magic word to say to make this right.

"It was a fun time," she said.

A tear trickled down Wren's cheek as she nodded.

"Incredibly … fun. Okay, kiss me here before I start bawling. Shit."

Amanda smiled and swept Wren into her arms. So many times during the last few days, Wren had been in control. Wren had been the one to take the lead, but she seemed incredibly fragile right then, so Amanda stepped up. That felt like how a relationship should be.

They kissed, and it was a messy affair, both of them sniffling and holding on too tight, but it was a balm to Amanda's heart. This New Year's had changed her life. It had changed her perspective. She would never be the same.

She pulled away, and Wren let her go, taking a swift step back.

"Talk soon?" Wren said.

"Very."

They stared at each other for an extra-long beat before Amanda turned on her heels and headed toward the lines for TSA screening.

She didn't look behind her as she walked away, knowing it would be too hard. While in the slow-moving line, a numbness settled over her body.

Moments from their days together flashed through her brain like a slideshow. She lingered on the ones that made her feel silly or bad because that was what brains did.

What was it that Wren had said? *I've always been written off for being out of control and wild.* Amanda knew Wren had had trouble in relationships because people didn't take her seriously. They didn't think she took life seriously, even though she practically had a lingerie empire, which didn't happen without a bunch of dedication and hard work.

What else? *I don't want to let the* fun, fun, fun *part of me dictate this.*

That was the piece that kept getting stuck in Amanda's mind, but it was suddenly knocked loose. Wren thought she was only worth a good time. She'd been told that, had felt it in others' actions. Then Amanda had spent days telling her how fucking fun she was! Amanda had probably made Wren worry this was all a nightmarish repeat.

Amanda ducked under the tape to get out of line and whipped out her cell phone.

Amanda: *Hey! Just so you know, that part of you that is wild, that likes to dance and go streaking and flash me in a karaoke bar. The part that gave me the best sex of my existence. That FUN part? I LOVE THAT PART.*

Amanda: *If you were in front of me, I'd be yelling that. I love that you're fun. That is not a part of you I'm going to write off. It is THE REASON I want to be with you. It's why, after a total of three days, I want to move across the country and open Myrna's Closet by Mount and be with you!*

Amanda: *OMG, I'm not sure if I'm making sense, but you make me so happy. You made me feel free and like myself for the first fucking time in my adult life. That light in you is the reason I want to be with you. And not in the short term. Not temporarily. Not as fuck buddies or a fling. I don't need time. I don't need for the sex haze to wear off. I know what I want.*

Amanda: *I wish you were here so I could say this to your* *face. I got out of line and everything. I wish I'd thought of these words before you'd left.*

Wren: *William's turning the car around. I'll be there in two minutes.*

Amanda: *William?*

Wren: *I asked him to follow us to the airport so I could cry in his car on the way home.*

Amanda: *Oh God, Wren.*

A tear dripped off Amanda's chin, and she laughed. Only finding the right thing to say to Wren via text was very *them*.

Amanda saw Wren storm through the door by the check-in desks. They hurried toward each other. Wren barreled right into Amanda's arms, and she didn't want to lose her chance to say her piece, so she started babbling.

"I want this. It's okay if you don't or if you're not certain. I can wait you out, Wren Rebello. But the very thing you're worried about, those facets of yourself that others have written off, they are some of the many, many, many reasons that make me care for you."

"Are you sure?" Wren asked, her face buried in Amanda's shoulder. "Please be sure. For so long, I've felt like one of those cheap party favors. Fun for a moment, easily discarded. I couldn't handle it if you viewed me that way."

"Oh, Wren. VIP party favors from here on out. *You* changed my life. I want this new life, not the stale, stagnant one I've been sleepwalking through. It doesn't have to be immediate. We can go slow, take our time, but this is the endgame. That's my goal. You're the endgame."

Wren laughed and squeezed Amanda harder. "Same-sies." She lifted her head and looked right at Amanda. "You still have to get on the plane, though."

Amanda nodded. "Yeah. I do. But I'll be heading back here eventually. To be with you." Amanda thumbed the tears off Wren's cheeks.

She felt aglow with possibility, a buffet of opportunities laid out in front of her. If this was what taking control of her life was like, she wanted to do it every freaking day.

Wren lifted Amanda's palm and kissed it. That was where she'd kissed Amanda at midnight too. It felt like a sign of good luck and good fortune.

Amanda hugged Wren close again. "This is going to be a very good year."

Epilogue

One Year Later

Wren: *Are you at the shop?*

Wren had left her apartment and was supposed to meet Amanda at Mount, but she knew her girlfriend. Recently, it had been nearly impossible to pull Amanda away from her as-of-yet unopened vintage clothing store.

Amanda: *Shit. Yes. I lost track of time. Just need to change clothes. I'll meet you outside.*

Wren smiled at her phone. Even after a year, texts from Amanda made her chest flutter.

Wren: *Sounds good.*

Amanda was working remotely for Ellis International Products, but she also had a permanent booth at a flea market downtown, where the hipsters ate her wares up, and was only one month away from the grand opening of Myrna's Closet. She was working her ass off.

Mount and Myrna's Closet were only a few blocks

from Wren's apartment, so it didn't take her long to turn the corner and see the colorful storefronts. Amanda was leaning against the orange wooden door of Myrna's wearing a gorgeous pale-blue silk jumpsuit with wide legs. It seemed like something out of the '70s, which meant it probably was. There was a long line of people on the other side of the street waiting to get into Mount.

As soon as Wren was within arm's length, Amanda kissed her swiftly. "Oh my God, you look amazing!"

Wren playfully preened. "My girlfriend gave me this jacket." Wren loved that word—*girlfriend*.

"I knew it would be perfect for you." Amanda walked a circle around Wren, taking in the outfit from all sides. Wren was wearing leather leggings, her favorite combat boots, and a bright yellow suit jacket from the '80s with nothing underneath. She'd used double-sided tape to keep the jacket in place and prevent any wardrobe malfunctions.

Wren snatched Amanda to her as she finished her circuit and kissed her neck. She marveled at the fact that she could kiss Amanda whenever she wanted, hold her, *see* her. Amanda had moved about seven months ago. Wren could have lasted longer doing the long-distance thing. She would have done it forever if it had meant being with Amanda over holiday weekends and vacations—that was love for you—but, man, was she thankful she got to see Amanda every day now.

They crossed the street hand in hand. The bouncer waved them in, which was a thrill in itself. Perks of knowing the owner, she supposed.

The crowd swept them in, so Wren gripped Amanda's hand tighter. They came to Mount pretty often to dance, to see friends, or for a nightcap when they were spending the night at Amanda's apartment, but tonight it was as rowdy as Wren had ever seen it.

Adrenaline zipped through her, ramping her up immediately. She spotted Benji and tugged Amanda in that direction. Benji threw his arms around Amanda and started chatting her ears off immediately. Wren watched them with a smile. They were thick as thieves. She greeted her other friends, who were posted up around the table. They had all accepted Amanda into their group like she was meant to be there, like she would have a place with them forever. And Wren hoped she did. Even if the worst happened and they didn't work out, she wanted Amanda in her life. She wanted Amanda to have a family here.

Of course, if Wren had any say in the matter, she and Amanda would be together forever.

"Benji said the hot bartender is making cocktails with sparklers in them," Amanda said excitedly in her ear. "Let's go!"

"That cannot be safe." Wren grinned. "Which I love. Lead the way."

At the bar, there were big buckets of party favors, including Ring Pops with tags that said, "Ring in the New Year." Amanda snagged one of the lollipops and stuck it on her own ring finger. They ordered the drink special for the night, called the Sparkly Midnight Kiss. The "hot bartender" lined up their Kisses on the edge of the bar and quickly lit the short sparkler garnish in both.

They were so fascinated by the sparklers that neither of them managed to snag their drink from the bar before the sparks had died off. It had only lasted about fifteen seconds.

Wren picked up her Sparkly Midnight Kiss with a laugh and *tink*ed her glass against Amanda's. "To the old year."

Amanda smiled. "To the old year. And the new."

"The new."

Amanda took a sip of her drink, and her eyes scrunched shut. "Fuck, that's sweet."

Wren laughed, tried hers, and shuddered at the overwhelming sugariness. "Yep. Bottoms up." She drank the rest in a few hearty swallows.

"Braver than me. I'm going to have to nurse this." Amanda pulled her out onto the dancefloor. She alternated between sips of her Midnight Kiss and lavish sucks on her Ring Pop, which turned Wren on way more than it should have.

The crowd was raucous, but there was a joyfulness in the air. Just a bunch of queer people enjoying the safety of a gay bar on New Year's Eve. Enjoying sugary drinks and dance music and the company of their friends.

They spent all night dancing. They danced with Benji and William, Rosie and Leo. Wren boogied down with Rosie and Benji's other sister, Sasha, and her husband, Perry. They slow danced with Robin and did the YMCA with women from the roller derby team. It wasn't Father

Time Farm and Resort. It wasn't fancy, but it was a wonderful night.

Hell, Wren would have been happy no matter where she was or what she was doing as long as it was with Amanda. It would have been an awesome New Year's even if they had been at home in their pajamas. Either of their homes.

Not living together yet worked for them. Wren thought they were being very responsible about that. Not rushing. Not being too rash.

But damn, as she threw her arms over Amanda's shoulders and brought her down for a kiss, she couldn't help but wish she got to wake up next to Amanda every morning. She dreamed of sharing one bed, one refrigerator, one mailbox with her.

Maybe that would come in time, and if it didn't, that was okay. But if she were being honest with herself—she wanted it. She just didn't want to push it.

As the evening wore on, Amanda became more and more disheveled. She'd acquired a party hat from a random person and had it perched off-kilter on her head. Noisemakers had been passed out at some point, and she had a large kazoo stuffed through the strap of her bra for easy access. She'd discarded her Ring Pop, but it had painted her mouth bright red. Her hair was tangled around her shoulders, and her face was rosy from dancing.

She was hot as fuck.

There must have been something in Wren's eyes that clued Amanda into her dirty thoughts because Amanda led Wren deeper into the writhing mass of people on the dancefloor where it was impossible to see where one person ended and another began. They were pressed close. It was incredibly public, but the crowd lent them anonymity and concealment.

Amanda kissed Wren hard. She tasted like fruity cocktails and a cherry sucker. The smell of sweat from other dancers wafted around them, but Wren was flooded with Amanda's unique amber-and-cinnamon scent. Without warning, Amanda slipped her hand into Wren's suit jacket and fingered her nipple piercing. Wren's knees almost gave out. She wasn't wearing a bra, so Amanda's access was totally unencumbered.

Wren moaned into Amanda's mouth and melted under her hands. She was wet, excited by the naughtiness of this and the pull and tug against her nipple.

She should have been worried that someone might see, but her jacket was covering her, so she didn't give a fuck. It felt too good. Wild and impulsive and perfect.

The sudden countdown to midnight made them both jump—Wren had had no idea what time it was—but they didn't stop kissing.

They kissed while the crowd chanted, "Ten ... Nine ... Eight ..."

Amanda snuck her hand into the opposite side of the jacket and rolled Wren's other nipple between her thumb and forefinger.

"Fuck, fuck," Wren said, having to gasp for breath.

"I love you," Amanda said, an ornery smile on her face.

"Five … Four …"

"I love you too, you slut."

Amanda threw her head back and laughed, but she managed to get her mouth back on Wren's by the time everyone yelled, "One! Happy New Year!"

They kissed for too long. Everyone around them had started to move again, hugging and toasting, and still they kissed. Eventually, Wren pulled back and said, "Your apartment. Now."

They made it over to Myrna's within minutes. "Want to see what I painted today?" Amanda asked.

"Of course." Wren was horny, but she would never stop Amanda from showing off her hard work.

Amanda led her over to the checkout counter, which had been painted mint green. Wren laughed. It looked amazing but was not what Wren had been expecting. Amanda had come into this business venture with a vision, but that vision surprised Wren every day. The racks of clothes were color-coordinated, causing a rainbow effect around the store. There were shelves of vintage patterns and display cases of jewelry and accessories. Amanda had also bought antique furniture for a sitting area and huge, gaudy mirrors for every corner. The walls were pale pink. Considering Amanda's own style was understated vintage, Wren was delighted by the kitschy brightness of her store. It made the place welcoming and fun.

"If that wasn't wet paint, I'd pin you to it and ravish you," Wren joked. "This place is going to be awesome. I'm so proud of you."

Amanda blushed. "I hope I don't crash and burn."

"You won't. And if you do, I'll be here to put the fire out and help you start over."

Amanda nodded, her eyes a little shiny. Wren squeezed her hand.

After one last glance around the store, they ran upstairs to Amanda's tiny apartment. While Amanda got them water, chattering away about their night, Wren sat at her kitchen table. Wren loved this table. It was much better than the IKEA one she used. Amanda had bought it at the flea market and refurbished it.

There were two pieces of paper sitting on the table, both lists. Wren recognized the paper. It was from the pad of dreams they'd gotten at that weird pyramid scheme workshop they'd snuck into last year.

Wren pulled the papers closer. They were lists of New Year's resolutions. Her smile grew as her eyes skimmed over the first one. It was the one written at the workshop, the one Amanda hadn't wanted to throw away. It had creases from where she'd folded it.

On it, Amanda had written out her dreams about opening a clothing store, changing jobs, finding independence, stepping outside the expectations of her family.

Wren snuck a peek at the other list. These resolutions must have been new. The pen was sitting by the pad.

- Make a home together (if Wren wants that).
- Get a cat.
- Convince Myrna to fly out to see the store.

Wren laughed. She and Amanda were on the same page about moving in together, but obviously neither of them knew how to broach the subject. Wren picked up the pen and scrawled "I do" next to the first resolution.

Amanda waltzed out of the kitchen and plopped the water down. They both drank it like they were starving but didn't say a word. She scattered her accumulated goodies over the table—the kazoo, the party hat, a box of champagne-flavored gummy bears. Cheap, fun things they would throw away tomorrow, but Wren had a new appreciation for party favors. Where there were party favors, there was normally a playful Amanda as well.

Watchful anticipation tinged the air. Finally, Wren said, "Take your clothes off, A. I'm going to wreck you. Teasing me like that at the club." She shook her head, pretending to be very stern.

Amanda stood up and very slowly unzipped her jumpsuit. It fluttered to the floor. Underneath, she was wearing silky strappy lingerie Wren had designed, which made a possessive greediness pulse through her.

Wren ripped off her jacket, shucked down her leather leggings, and fell to her knees. She very carefully helped Amanda out of her panties. With a steadying hand, she led one of Amanda's feet up onto the kitchen chair, then scooted until she could reach Amanda's pussy with her mouth.

They didn't do it standing up that often, but there was something extremely fulfilling about being on her knees for Amanda. At worshipping her pretty cunt with lips and teeth and tongue.

Wren took her time, bringing Amanda to the edge once, then twice more, stopping every few minutes to finger fuck her hard, lick the juices off the inside of her thighs, and whisper dirty things against her skin.

"Please, Wren. I need it," Amanda gasped.

"What do you need, love? Wanna hear you say it."

"*You*. Make me come, please."

Arousal bolted through Wren. She loved hearing Amanda beg. She loved the way Amanda's legs were shaking and the way she gripped Wren's head to her pussy like that would do any lick of good.

Wren slipped three fingers into Amanda's slick cunt. Amanda threw her head back and moaned.

"Don't come yet," Wren warned.

"Can't … Oh fuck." Amanda shook her head. Her pussy squeezed around Wren's fingers.

"*Amanda*. I said not to come." Wren smiled. She knew the command in her voice was a lost cause. Amanda was definitely about to orgasm. It turned them both on too much when she couldn't hold it back.

"I'm going to. Oh fuck, Wren." Amanda's hand slammed down on the kitchen table to hold herself up, and Wren heard the crinkling of paper. She gave one last suck to Amanda's clit, which set Amanda off in all the ways Wren loved. Amanda's arousal dripped down Wren's fingers, and Amanda moaned brokenly. Wren lapped lightly at Amanda's clit while the aftershocks wore off.

After Wren sat back to catch her breath, Amanda opened her eyes blearily. Wren noticed that Amanda's

New Year's resolutions for this year were crumpled under her hand. "Hey, be careful there, pretty girl. Don't want to ruin your list. It's important."

Amanda blinked down at the paper before straightening it, smoothing out the wrinkles. Wren smiled as Amanda's eyes went wide, and she leaned down to get a better look, clearly clocking what Wren had written earlier.

"Really?" Amanda asked, her voice shaky and full of hope.

"New year, new home together, I always say."

The happiness in Amanda's smile was as sweet as champagne, and Wren would cherish it forever.

More So Over the Holidays

Did you miss Books 1-3 in the So Over the Holidays series? Check them out now for more queer, raunchy, fluffy, holiday fun!

Stocking Stuffers (So Over the Holidays #1)

Sasha Holiday is so over the holidays after getting left at the altar last Christmas Eve. But as the marketing maven for Lady Robin's Intimate Implements, she's stuck not-so-merrily pitching naughty toys at a romance book club's Christmas party. Her loathing of the yuletide only intensifies as a snowstorm rolls in and traps her at the Winterberry Inn. Stranded with her is Perry Winters—a hot bearded book club member trimmed in flannel and tattoos.

Perry's a romantic with an unerring belief in the magic of the season, and he recognizes a Christmas miracle when he sees it. Brave, smart, and confident—Sasha Holiday is a gift. And the gifts keep coming when she suggests they pass the time with some no-strings fun. After all, she has a big bag of toys that would make even Santa want to stay in bed on Christmas Eve.

But the frisky festivities turn complicated as feelings spark between Sasha and Perry. Perry wants to see Sasha once the snow clears, but Sasha is reluctant to take the relationship sleigh ride again. Perry will have to show her that love is more than just a holiday feeling.

Candy Hearts (So Over the Holidays #2)

Mechanic Benji Holiday is so over Valentine's Day and men who don't get him. A weekend getaway with friends to escape the holiday hubbub is exactly what he needs. But William O'Dare—a stern and silent nightclub owner with "Be My Valentine" practically stamped on his forehead—throws a wrench into Benji's plans.

William has spent years focused on his career, and it has cost him friendships and love. Inexperienced in the business of romance, he's on the hunt for the perfect partner, and he's armed with specific criteria to guide him. But William didn't expect a hunky mechanic wrapped in satin and lace to show up on his doorstep.

Unable to resist their attraction, Benji and William agree to be secret fake valentines for the weekend, but secrets have a way of getting out. William gets struck by Cupid's arrow, and as the weekend winds down, he doesn't want fake or secret. He wants Benji to be his valentine for real and for keeps.

Candy Hearts is a male/male Valentine's Day novella featuring a house party power outage, meddling friends and siblings, naughty lingerie and naughtier toys, homemade Valentine's Day cards, and a happily ever after.

Bottle Rocket (So Over the Holidays #3)

Freshly single Rosie Holiday is on the hunt for passion and excitement. This leads her to Leo Whittaker—a bad boy who waltzed out of town, and her life, thirteen years ago. Leo isn't the type to stick around, but Rosie's not going to let a no-strings opportunity pass her by.

When a business trip sends Leo back to his hometown, the last thing he expects is for his first love to hand him a list of scorching-hot escapades and a deadline. He's happy to help Rosie discover her bossy side in the bedroom. Or in a fireworks stand. Or at a Fourth of July barbecue.

Their chemistry burns bright and fast, but what tore them apart years ago is still between them. They are polar opposites. A reserved kindergarten teacher and an irreverent artist. A nester and a wanderer. It will take a spark of imagination and a lot of love to keep their second-chance romance from flaming out.

Also by Erin McLellan

Did you enjoy *Party Favors*? Try one of these stories by Erin McLellan next!

If you like to read small-town romance:

- *Life on Pause* (Love Life #1)
- *Small City Heart*

If you like angsty romance:

- *Controlled Burn* (Farm College #1)
- *Clean Break* (Farm College #2)

If you like fun, fluffy, and hot:

- *Stocking Stuffers* (So Over the Holidays #1)
- *Candy Hearts* (So Over the Holidays #2)
- *Bottle Rocket* (So Over the Holidays #3)
- *Life of Bliss* (Love Life #2)

If you like action and adventure:

- *Natural Disaster* (Storm Chasers #1)

Acknowledgments

Thank you so much to all the So Over the Holidays readers. Your support made it possible to move this series from the Holiday siblings to their friends. I'll forever be thankful for your enthusiasm.

All the cheers go to Susie Selva for her impeccable editing, M.A. Hinkle for eagle-eyed proofreading, Cate Ashwood for another perfect cover, and Judith & Linn at A Novel Take PR for the great promo. Big socially distanced hugs to Karen, Allison, Layla, and Lisa for cheering me one while writing this book. A big thanks to my local friends for brainstorming titles with me, and an extra salute to Susie for help with my blurb.

Lastly, hugs and kisses to my family.

About the Author

Erin McLellan is the author of the Farm College, So Over the Holidays, and Storm Chasers series. She enjoys writing happily ever afters that are earthy, emotional, quirky, humorous, and very sexy. Originally from Oklahoma, she currently lives in Alaska and spends her time dreaming up queer contemporary romances. She is a lover of chocolate, college sports, antiquing, Dr Pepper, and binge-worthy TV shows.

CPSIA information can be obtained
at www.ICGtesting.com
Printed in the USA
LVHW092052021221
705095LV00008B/1273

9 781735 004938